Exit the Body

A Farce in Three Acts

by Fred Carmichael

A SAMUEL FRENCH ACTING EDITION

New York Hollywood London Toronto

SAMUELFRENCH.COM

STORY OF THE PLAY

Here is a new farce mystery that was greeted with unanimous rave notices when premiered in Summer Stock. "Hilarious, delicious, uproarious, hysterical—pick your own adjective . . . first night audience howled, guffawed, roared and applauded."—*Bennington (Vt.) Banner*. "Never have tears of laughter flowed so freely . . . even conservative New Englanders howled."—*Rutland (Vt.) Herald*. ". . . delightful romp . . . always witty, often excruciatingly funny."—*Williamstown (Mass.) News*. "Roars of laughter."—*Pelham (N. Y.) Sun*. The story tells of a woman mystery writer who rents a New England house which was supposed to be the rendezvous point for some stolen jewels. The focal point of the set is the closet which opens into a living room and into a library. In the closet is found a body which promptly disappears only to be succeeded by a second body. The hunt for the jewels reaches a climax at Two A. M. when four couples. all unknown to each other, turn up to search. Not since the days of Mack Sennett has there been such an hilarious series of entrances and exits. The leading roles of the writer, her secretary, and the local maid give actresses a field day. Two of the male characters are small parts and the rest of the cast is equal in size and humor. From the opening laugh to the final line, this is guaranteed to make even the most staid audience cry with laughter.

EXIT THE BODY was first presented in Summer Stock at the Dorset Playhouse, Dorset, Vermont, on August 31, 1961.

EXIT THE BODY
by Fred Carmichael
Staged by The Author
Scenic Design by Judith Page Murray

(Cast in order of their appearance)

LILLIAN SEYMOUR	*Lynnette Mettey*
JENNY	*Ann Laurence*
RANDOLPH	*Charles Dickens*
HELEN O'TOOLE	*Linda Brown Rue*
KATE BIXLEY	*Patricia Wyn Rose*
CRANE HAMMOND	*Polly Welch*
VERNON COOKLEY	*Frederick Edell*
LYLE ROGERS	*David Vacheron*
PHILIP SMITH	*William Mehegan*
RICHARD HAMMOND	*Barry Dunleavey*

The action of the play takes place in the living room of a New England home. TIME: The present.

ACT ONE
Afternoon on the first of August.

ACT TWO
After dinner that same evening.

ACT THREE
Two A.M. the following morning.

The author wishes to thank Susan M. Richardson for her help and assistance in making the opening in Dorset, Vermont, the most successful in the company's history.

Exit the Body

ACT ONE

SCENE: *The entire action of the play takes place in the living room of a New England house which has been rented for the month of August. The room is very tastefully furnished and the decor shows that an experienced and high-priced interior decorator has been at work. The walls are painted a light, bright summer color or possibly paneled. The portion of the entrance hallway which is visible has wallpaper covering it. Down Right is a small straightbacked chair with arms; immediately above it are French doors leading off Right and showing that the house is situated on a hill. In the Up Right corner is a whatnot with various copper and brass articles on it, the only workable prop being a silent butler. Up Right on the back wall and slightly towards Center is a closet, the door of which opens into the room and to the Right. The interior of the closet is painted a lighter shade of the room color so that it will be a focal point when the door is open. Inside the closet are a row of hooks on the back wall and a door on the Right wall leading into the library. NOTE: It is important that the audience have a complete view of the closet at all times. Immediately to the Left of the closet a small wall goes Upstage. This wall forms the outside wall of the closet and also the wall of the hallway. Between this wall and the far Upstage wall of the house is a passageway leading Off Right to the library, hence the library may be approached from either the inner closet door or the hallway. Directly Up Center on the back wall is a door opening Onstage and to the Right which leads to the outside. To the Left of this door is a stairway leading to the upper portions of the house. The entire hallway is framed by an archway from the living room. Upstage Left is a bookcase built into the wall. The top shelves are filled with bric-a-brac and the bottom two shelves serve as a bar; they are lined with glasses, bottles, etc. The Left wall runs down to a swinging kitchen door which is Down Left. The furniture in the room consists of a two-seater sofa, Right near the French doors, a small table is to the Right of it; a small stuffed armchair Center, with a small table to the Right of it, and a desk, flat-topped, Left. This desk is almost perpendicular to the audience and has an ash tray on top of it, a telephone Upstage on it, and, at the moment, a large gingham flower in a bud-vase. There is a small desk lamp on the Upstage end of the desk, and a chair pushed into it on the Left side, so that anyone sitting there faces the room. Since this play is a farce, the colors should be bright and gay and the sunlight which streams through the French doors a warm, summer yellow.*

At-Rise: Lillian *is just closing the closet door.* Lillian *is an attractive woman, exceedingly well-dressed since she is a top-flight designer. Her age is indeterminate but she is a contemporary of* Crane's. *These two parts may be played anywhere from the thirties to the fifties.* Lillian *pats the closet door as if she has accomplished a job. She silently tip-toes toward the front door when the PHONE on the desk rings. She automatically heads for it but suddenly realizes this is not her house. She runs for the front door, opens it and starts out, but she sees someone coming from Off Left, closes the door, looks around frantically for an exit and decides upon the French doors. She runs out through them and closes them behind her. Just as they close, the front door opens and* Jenny *pokes her head in.* Jenny *is a young country girl dressed in a rather gaudy and inexpensive cotton. Her hair may be worn in pig-*

*tails or a pony-tail. She is rather loud but the epit-
ome of innocence. Her age must be between eighteen
and twenty-five.* JENNY *comes into the room leaving
the door open. She looks around and calls:*

JENNY. Mrs. Hammond! (*She starts upstairs and calls
again, louder.*) Mrs. Hammond! You here or ain't you?
Guess not. (*Turns to the front door.*) Randolph, it's O.K.
No one's here yet.

(RANDOLPH *pokes his head in. He is a cheap crook and
proud of it. He has tried to look like television's idea
of a hoodlum and has almost succeeded. He has a
pencil-thin moustache, slicked-down hair, and wears
a very flashy sport coat with a dark shirt and bright
tie. His speech is not the best and he is determined
to work at it until he becomes a top crook. At the
moment, he is rather nervous.*)

RANDOLPH. You sure?
JENNY. She don't answer.
RANDOLPH. Her plane landed forty-five minutes ago.
She oughta be here soon.
JENNY. (*As she pulls* RANDOLPH *in and shuts the
door.*) Vernon is driving her.
RANDOLPH. So?
JENNY. With his driving and his car, she won't be here
for ages.
RANDOLPH. (*Comes into the living room and looks over
the house.*) Geez, this is some layout.
JENNY. There's lots of houses in the village just as
nice. People that owns 'em fixes 'em up for the summer
and then they go to Europe.
RANDOLPH. (*Crosses to the French doors and looks
out.*) And this Hammond dame has it for the next
month?
JENNY. (*Moves to between chair and sofa.*) Yeah—
Mr. Redfax had paid through the first—he could have
lived here up till yesterday.

RANDOLPH. (*Turns.*) Well, he ain't livin' nowheres now.

JENNY. I bet he was drinkin'. "If you drink, don't drive!" That's what they say.

RANDOLPH. If he wouldn't have crashed himself dead, we wouldn't have a job, would we?

JENNY. (*Sits in chair Center.*) Gee, that's right.

RANDOLPH. (*Crosses to* JENNY *and pulls her up.*) Well, come on. Show me the joint. If I gotta do a job while the Hammond woman is living here, I want to know where I'm workin'.

JENNY. (*Goes to kitchen door and holds it open for him.*) This is my room—the kitchen. (RANDOLPH *goes into the kitchen below* JENNY.) This is where I cooked poor Mr. Redfax his last supper. Makes me feel kinda sad I didn't do better. If I'da known he was goin' to die, I would never have used instant coffee. I'd a percolated.

RANDOLPH. (*Comes out of kitchen, pats her cheek and crosses to the stairs.*) You're a real decent girl, Jenny. Upstairs just bedrooms, huh?

JENNY. Yeah.

RANDOLPH. Where's this lead to? (*He goes off Right to the library.*)

JENNY. (*Follows him to Up Center.*) Library. It's full of books. Mr. Redfax never read nothin' except that racin' form he got in the mail.

RANDOLPH. (*Offstage.*) He had his fingers in more rackets—everything from juke boxes to dope. (*He re-enters and comes Down to the arch.*) What a joint! Hey, it's furnished right down to the booze. (*Crosses to the bar and picks up a bottle of Scotch.*)

JENNY. Everything. They even have salt in the salt shakers. That's why the rent's so high. (*Takes bottle from him.*) I don't think you should touch that liquor, Randolph. It's illegal.

RANDOLPH. (*Grabs bottle back again.*) So is breaking and entering. (*Pours himself a shot.*)

JENNY. We didn't break and I have a right to enter. I work here.

RANDOLPH. You want a shot?

JENNY. Not me.

RANDOLPH. (*Toasts* JENNY.) Boy, this is the life! (*Drinks.*)

JENNY. I guess Mrs. Hammond is rich. She's a good writer, huh?

RANDOLPH. The greatest. Never less than five murders in her books. And as for sex— (*He nudges* JENNY *and she giggles.*) You see more of her books on the subways than you do the Daily News.

JENNY. And I'll be workin' for her.

RANDOLPH. Might as well have another little one. Can't fly on one wing. (*He pours another shot and laughs at his joke.*)

JENNY. A helicopter has no wings.

RANDOLPH. (*Freezes with the bottle thinking this over.*) I don't follow that at all. (*Leaves bottle on desk, crosses and sits in chair Center.*) Ah, this is the life for me. When we get our split from the Boss, this is how we'll live.

JENNY. (*Moves to his Left.*) But suppose the diamonds ain't here?

RANDOLPH. They gotta be. After the heist was made in New York, the ice was brought out here.

JENNY. But what about the diamonds?

RANDOLPH. Pigeon, ice is diamonds. That's the way you gotta talk now you're turnin' crooked.

JENNY. I'll try.

RANDOLPH. Now the fence—

JENNY. (*Pleased to know this.*) That's the person who buys the stolen ice.

RANDOLPH. Now you're catchin' on, pigeon. The fence comes to pick up the ice, but Redfax gets killed before he can turn them over. So, the diamonds gotta be *here.*

JENNY. And I can search while I clean up the house—

RANDOLPH. And at night, you can let me in and we'll look together. (*He pulls* JENNY *onto his lap.*) A perfect set-up. The Boss is no fool.

JENNY. But I don't even know the Boss. When am I going to get introduced? Who signs my W–2 form?

RANDOLPH. Pigeon, this is not declarable income.

JENNY. Gee, that's great. But I like to know who I'm workin' for.

RANDOLPH. (*Pushes her up.*) Get us the bottle, huh?

JENNY. (*Gets bottle from desk.*) Hadn't you better start lookin' for the ice? (*Starts for front door.*) They'll be here—they'll be here soon.

RANDOLPH. In a minute. Sure a lucky thing I sat next to you at the movies. I mean, out of all the girls in Birchville, I should have slipped my arm around the one who works in this house.

JENNY. (*Comes down to his Right.*) I don't usually let strangers do that in the picture shows, you know. But I could tell you was a gentleman. (*Hands him the bottle.*)

RANDOLPH. (*Pours a drink.*) My mother brung me up right. She trained me to go crooked just like other kid's moms train them to go straight. When I was only a little kid, she ran a hot dog stand on the beach and she taught me how to go up behind little girls after they'd bought a hot dog and reach over their shoulder and pull the hot dog out of the bun. Then I'd give it back to Mom. It was great. All summer we only used three dozen hot dogs and twenty-five hundred buns. (*Rises and drinks.*) I tried it with hamburgers but they come apart. (*Crosses and puts the bottle down on the bar.*)

JENNY. What's your mother doing now?

RANDOLPH. (*Turns at the bar.*) Ten years.

JENNY. Why?

RANDOLPH. (*Sits on the Center side of desk, on the top.*) She lifted an emerald necklace off a dame at the opera. Mother loves Bizet. (*He pronounces it with a hard "t."*) She took the necklace just as Carmen was tryin' to sell her cigarettes.

JENNY. (*Moves to* RANDOLPH.) But they caught her?

RANDOLPH. Yeah—she couldn't resist wearin' the emeralds. They picked her up at the Automat on 46th Street. (*Pulls* JENNY *in to him.*) You know the last thing

Mother said to me as they took her away? She said, "Randolph, by the time I come out, I hope you're wanted!" Really had faith in me.

JENNY. I guess she must be proud of you now.

RANDOLPH. (*Rises and crosses to the Left of the desk and rummages through the drawers during the next speeches.*) I ain't done so well lately. When I met up with the Boss, I was smuggling Mexicans across the border at Tijuana. Used to drive them right by the customs inspectors. I had them stuffed inside a big wicker hamper.

JENNY. And the authorities never looked in?

RANDOLPH. I said I was a snake charmer. But one of them Mexicans was a louse. Instead of paying me off, he mugged me and stole my car. But then I ran into the Boss and I said, "Any time you want a job done, give me a ring." (*Crosses below desk and sits on Downstage side of it.*) So here I am relaxing in New England about to grab a fistful of diamonds and retire.

JENNY. (*Moves down to* RANDOLPH.) Nothing exciting's ever happened to me. I worked downstate around home and then finally my Ma said I ought to see something of the world. So this summer I come up here. But it's the same upstate as it is downstate except the sap runs later.

RANDOLPH. I'll show you the world, pigeon. I may even take you to Boston.

JENNY. (*Pulls him up.*) Gee, let's look for the diamonds right now.

RANDOLPH. Plenty of time. (*Pulls her in to him.*) Just you and me here like this is pretty nice.

JENNY. (*Just as he starts to kiss her.*) I hear a car! (*Runs to the front door.*)

RANDOLPH. We can come back when they're asleep. (*Crosses Upstage between sofa and chair.*)

JENNY. (*Peeks out door.*) It's them. (*Closes door.*)

RANDOLPH. Out this way. (*Heads for French doors.*)

JENNY. (*As she runs to him.*) Go to the left and they won't see us. (*They are almost out when* JENNY *speaks.*) Oh, your glass! (*Runs back to pick it up on the desk.*)

RANDOLPH. Bring it with you. (*Waits for her by windows.*)

JENNY. Run! (*They are out of sight just as the front door opens.* HELEN O'TOOLE *backs into the room talking to people outside.* HELEN *is a very efficient real estate saleswoman, perhaps a trifle too folsky and straight-laced at times but she means well. She carries a purse and wears a rather severe summer dress with an almost peculiar hat perched on her head.*)

HELEN. I knew you'd just love every little bit of it, Mrs. Hammond. Wait until you see the inside. It's a dream.

CRANE. (*Offstage.*) Look, Kate, a garden. Don't you adore flowers?

KATE. (*Offstage.*) Only four roses. I pray we have a bar.

HELEN. (*Hurt, she turns and crosses to the Right of the arch, speaking almost to herself.*) The house is fully equipped.

CRANE. (*Offstage.*) Oh, Kate, this is heavenly. Just look at the view.

KATE. I'm still car-sick. (*On this line,* KATE BIXLEY *has entered and leans against the door jamb.* KATE *is slightly older than* CRANE *and, being a secretary, she is dressed in a more tailored outfit. She has an irrepressible sense of humor that often borders on the sarcastic, but she doesn't really mean it.* KATE *and* CRANE *have a wonderful relationship, more that of friends than boss and secretary.* KATE *is wearing sun glasses, a traveling outfit, hat, and she carries a purse and fancy briefcase.*) I never thought we'd get here. I'm just a secretary, Miss O'Toole. A good, honest, New York secretary. Trees scare me.

HELEN. You'll get used to them, Miss—what was it again?

KATE. Bixley. (*She removes her sun glasses and crosses to the desk where she places the briefcase on the floor, the glasses in the purse, and her hat in a desk drawer.*) But you might as well call me Kate. Everyone does.

HELEN. (*Crosses to* KATE *and speaks barely above a*

whisper.) I'm so upset and nervous. I do hope Mrs. Hammond will like the house. It's a real estate agent's nightmare a client will hate what she hasn't seen.

KATE. Don't worry, she'll love it. She needs a place to rest up awhile and then write. This'll do just fine.

HELEN. (*With a glance to the door.*) I wish she'd come in and look at it.

KATE. (*Crosses to front door and calls Off Left.*) Crane, we're going to be living indoors. Aren't you curious? (*She moves to Right of arch.*)

CRANE. Coming, Kate. (CRANE HAMMOND *enters. She is the type of woman one likes immediately. She is attractive and possesses charm to the highest degree. She is bright, gay, and witty, an altogether likeable person. She is dressed in a smart traveling outfit with a coat over her shoulders. At the moment she is bubbling over with enthusiasm.*) I haven't seen so much green since St. Patrick's Day. I adore it, Kate. Isn't it heaven?

KATE. What happens at night? I don't see any streetlights.

CRANE. (*Crosses to* HELEN.) Kate, you'll learn to love the country. Imagine, Miss O'Toole, she's spent her whole life in New York and has never ever been to New England.

KATE. I've never ever been to Grant's Tomb.

CRANE. New Yorkers hate to travel.

HELEN. (*Moves to* KATE *and* CRANE *puts her bag on the desk.*) I bet you enjoyed the plane trip today, though —going through all those clouds.

KATE. (*One arm leaning on the arch.*) I was miserable. I even get sick at the Hayden Planetarium.

CRANE. (*Moves to* HELEN.) You're not going to kill my vacation. Miss O'Toole, I think it's perfect—the whole place. It's ideal.

HELEN. Well, I don't mind saying, Mrs. Hammond, it's a relief. I've never rented to anyone famous before and I thought you'd be—you know, finicky. I've only been in the business since June. As a matter of fact, Miss Seymour's house was the first commission I got.

CRANE. Oh, where is it? She said it was close. (*Goes to the French doors, crossing above the sofa.* HELEN *follows her.*)

HELEN. Just down the hill to the left.

CRANE. Imagine, Kate, having Lillian right next door.

KATE. What about our luggage? Do you think Goliath can handle it?

HELEN. (*Offended at* KATE's *inference.*) *Mr.* Cookley will attend to it. Don't worry.

CRANE. That's the country for you, Kate. Mr. Cookley meets us at the airport, drives us here and carries the luggage in. And I bet he'd even milk the cows for us, wouldn't he, Miss O'Toole?

HELEN. He won the contest last May—ninety-seven squirts to the minute.

(HELEN *points over* CRANE's *shoulder out the French doors in the direction of* LILLIAN's *house.* VERNON COOKLEY *enters carrying quite a load of luggage.* VERNON *is a middle-aged New Englander who has never seen any more of the country than ten miles outside of Birchville. He rarely lets an expression creep over his face and, in true New England fashion, is leery of everyone and everything. He is dressed in rumpled slacks, a plaid shirt, a vest, and a battered fedora. He wears glasses and speaks with a New England twang. He walks up behind* KATE.)

VERNON. You want these upstairs?

KATE. (*Startled.*) Please. Sure you don't need help?

VERNON. Who from?

KATE. Sorry.

VERNON. (*As he goes upstairs.*) Only stayin' the month. Don't know what they want all this stuff for. (KATE *goes to the desk and takes a small notepad and pencil from her purse and records the trip expenses.*)

CRANE. I can just see the Indians out there and revolutionary men marching. How old is the house?

HELEN. The main part is pre-revolutionary.

CRANE. (*Moves below the sofa.*) Did George Washington sleep here?

HELEN. He could have.

KATE. I hope they turned the mattress.

HELEN. (*Laughs.*) Mrs. Hammond, there's something I have to tell you.

CRANE. (*Sits on the sofa.*) They've raised the rent.

HELEN. I know you'll understand what I'm going to tell you; I mean being a mystery writer and all. (*Moves to below the sofa.*) You know I read your "Cops and the Corpse" three times. I liked it so much I gave it up for Lent. Anyway, death and all that sort of thing doesn't bother you, does it?

CRANE. You mean natural or unnatural?

HELEN. Oh, most natural. You see, Marco Redfax, the gentleman who rented this house for July, was killed in his car. Had a blowout and went over the bridge (*Indicates out French doors.*) down past Grundy's farm.

CRANE. Oh, I'm sorry.

VERNON. (*Who has just come downstairs.*) No one else is. He was a crook. (*He goes out front door.*)

HELEN. (*Crosses above sofa to Left of* CRANE.) I'm afraid Verne's right, Mrs. Hammond. There was police all over the place. He was wanted for armed robbery. He stole the Rodney Williston jewel collection. They found everything but the diamonds. The police think he was supposed to come here and give the diamonds to a gate.

CRANE. It's a fence.

HELEN. Fence?

CRANE. Fence. He's the one who gets the stolen property and sells it.

HELEN. Well, I guess you ought to know.

KATE. (*Sits at the desk.*) To the point. Did the gate show up?

HELEN. (*Moves over to* KATE.) Nope. Leastways, not before the accident. Or else he was here but didn't get the jewels yet. The robbery was only just before Mr. Redfax was killed. (*Moves back to* CRANE.) The police went over this place with a fine-tooth comb and couldn't find the diamonds. They thought for sure he'd hidden them here.

KATE. Maybe they weren't in the house. Did they look in the baggage-room at the station?

VERNON. (*Has just entered from outside with more luggage.*) Couldn't.

KATE. Why not?

VERNON. No station. (*He goes upstairs.*)

HELEN. They couldn't find a thing. (*Sits in chair Center.*) But that's all over now and the town is settled back to peace and quiet just like the brochure says. But I just thought you should know.

KATE. (*Rises and moves to* HELEN.) Anything else cheery happen this summer? May Queen strangle in the Maypole?

CRANE. Thanks for telling me, Miss O'Toole. It doesn't bother me in the least. I just want to relax for one week and then work for three. That's my schedule.

HELEN. Another book?

CRANE. A TV series.

HELEN. Won't they censor it? I mean your writing is rather—well— (*Looks at* KATE.) the library doesn't carry it.

CRANE. Don't worry. I write differently for different mediums.

HELEN. And your husband's going to join you here? I can't wait to meet him.

CRANE. Next week—after the convention's over.

HELEN. What does he do?

CRANE. (*Freezes for a moment, looks at* KATE *who clears her throat.*) He's a writer, too, of sorts.

HELEN. How thrilling.

KATE. (*Starts crossing to above* CRANE, *obviously enjoying this.*) Not as hard-hitting as Mrs. Hammond, though.

HELEN. Really?

CRANE. He's working on a novel and in the meantime he's writing a newspaper column to tide him over.

HELEN. (*Eagerly.*) He's not Ed Sullivan?

CRANE. No.

HELEN. Walter Winchell?

CRANE. No.

HELEN. Who?

KATE. (*Leaning over* CRANE.) Tell the little lady.

CRANE. He's Dorothy Duckworth.

HELEN. *He* is.

CRANE. Someone has to write lonely heart columns. It pays very well.

HELEN. Yes, of course.

VERNON. (*Having come downstairs.*) I wrote her once. I had some money saved up. Asked her if I should get married to the girl I was courtin' or if I should buy another six cows.

KATE. What did she say?

VERNON. Buy a bull. Then, when you have all the cows you want, get married.

KATE. Did you?

VERNON. Bull died. Girl married my brother. You ready to go back now, Helen? Won't charge you the regular taxi fare. It's downhill.

HELEN. Right there, Verne. (VERNON *exits and* HELEN *rises and starts for the door.*) Well, I certainly do hope you ladies enjoy the house. Oh, I want to bring around my copy of your "Corpse in the Torn Nightgown" for you to autograph.

CRANE. (*Moves up to* HELEN's *Right.*) I'd love to.

HELEN. And if you should happen to come upon those diamonds, just call the local sheriff. Don't get mixed up with any gates. (*She goes out and off Left.*)

CRANE. (*Closes the door.*) They're both so nice.

KATE. (*Imitating New England type.*) Real folks. (*Crosses below sofa.*) Once that car goes, we're trapped.

CRANE. I'll rent one for the month. (*Comes to* KATE *and throws her arms around her happily.*) Oh, Kate, isn't this marvelous? Just think—a whole week to relax and just look at the view and breathe that air.

KATE. Wait! (*Faces front.*) Listen, Crane!

CRANE. What? I don't hear a thing.

KATE. That's just the point. There's nothing to listen to. (*Sits on the sofa.*) No television, no radio, not even any traffic. At least I thought they'd have a phonograph. Now I can't even play my record of Times Square crowd noises.

CRANE. I'll convert you yet. (*Moves Center.*) By the end of the month, you'll be dressed in a sunbonnet and drinking nothing stronger than milk.

KATE. (*With a milking gesture.*) Straight from the tap.

CRANE. (*Notices the gingham flower on the desk.*) Well, look at that.

KATE. Fake flowers in the country. Tsk! Tsk!

CRANE. (*Reads card attached to flower.*) "Welcome, darling. This is direct from Lord and Taylor. Have some wonderful surprises for you. Lillian." Count on Lillian for the unexpected.

KATE. Her biggest joke was getting us to come here.

CRANE. It's perfect. With Richard at the convention and Kathy being a counselor at camp, there was no use hanging around New York.

KATE. We had air-conditioning.

CRANE. This house is air-conditioned by God.

KATE. It's hot, by God.

CRANE. It's summer.

KATE. (*Rises and crosses to* CRANE.) I'm only kidding, Crane. I'm sure I'll get to love it.

CRANE. Well, let's unpack.

KATE. First, I want to investigate the kitchen. If the local maid is anything like Vernon Cookley, I may end up defrosting supper. (*She goes into kitchen.*)

CRANE. I'll hang up the coats and things. (*Picks up her coat and heads for the closet. As she opens the closet door, the view attracts her attention and she looks out windows while still holding onto the open closet door. Inside the closet we see a body hanging on a hook. It is the body of a very attractive man who is dressed in slacks, sport coat, sport shirt and a maroon ascot at the neck. He is leaning forward.* NOTE: *It is essential that the entire audience be able to see the body.*) Oh, the country.

KATE. (*After a moment, calls from Offstage.*) Crane. Come here.

CRANE. (*Dumps coat on back of sofa and closes closet door without seeing the body. She goes to the kitchen.*) Did you find a cow in the kitchen?

KATE. (*Enters.*) Guess what? An electric refrigerator and we have running water. I envisioned myself manning the pumps before I could bathe.

CRANE. You've been seeing too many Westerns. Do you think Lillian would get us into anything prehistoric?

KATE. You said she had a sense of humor. I'll explore upstairs and you stand here and breathe that air. (*As she starts upstairs.*) Who knows? If my luck runneth good, I might even find an indoor john.

CRANE. (*Opens the closet door, gets the coat from the sofa, and is just about to turn to the closet when the PHONE rings. She puts down the coat, closes the closet door without seeing the body, crosses and picks up the phone.*) Hello—Lillian!—Yes, we made it right on schedule— No, everything's fine and we adored your flower. So thoughtful. When are we going to see you?— Sure, the house is stocked with everything, including Scotch. Come on up. Say, what's your surprise?—All right, I can wait. See you in a few minutes. (*Hangs up and goes to the foot of the stairs where she calls up to* KATE.) Lillian's coming over.

KATE. (*Offstage.*) Good. That means we can have a drink.

CRANE. This is vacation, Kate.

KATE. (*Comes part way downstairs.*) Guess what I found now?

CRANE. Martha Washington?

KATE. No, beds and bureaus and traces of civilization. But from the windows nothing. And I mean nothing. Acres and acres of it. The population explosion hasn't hit New England yet. (*She runs upstairs.*)

CRANE. They all move to the city. (*Picks up briefcase, crosses to closet, opens the door and throws briefcase in without seeing body, turns and gets coat from sofa, turns back to closet. She has left hand on closet door and right hand holding coat when she sees the body. She freezes, closes door, turns, and falls in a dead faint. The quicker the faint and the faster she hits the floor the better.)*

KATE. (*After a moment she comes downstairs and sees* CRANE *lying on the floor.*) I had no idea you were so tired. (*Crosses to her.*) Crane, I told you I found beds upstairs. Crane! Are you kidding? (CRANE *stirs.*) Honey, what happened?

CRANE. Closet! Don't go in the closet!

KATE. Of course I won't. Can you stand?

CRANE. Yes, but— (KATE *helps her up.*)

KATE. Come on over here and rest.

CRANE. Kate, promise me you won't go in that closet.

KATE. You mean never?

CRANE. (*As* KATE *sits her on sofa.*) There's a dead body in there.

KATE. Here, Crane, put your feet up. (*Helps her to do so.*) It'll be all right.

CRANE. I mean it. There is a body in our closet.

KATE. (*Picks up the coat* CRANE *dropped and puts it over back of sofa.*) You've been reading too many of your own books.

CRANE. Call the police. The Marshal. The Sheriff. Whoever the hell you call in the country.

KATE. I knew you were working too hard. I have the cutest psychiatrist on 86th Street.

CRANE. Call the police!

KATE. (*Starts to massage* CRANE'S *head at Right of sofa.*) Now, Crane, since you're lying down, why don't you tell me about your dreams?

CRANE. Well, last night, I—oh, Kate, stop it. (*Rises.*) There is a murdered man in our closet.

KATE. What's he doing there?

CRANE. Hanging on a hook.

KATE. Coat hanger or no?

CRANE. No.

KATE. Oh.

CRANE. (*Moves to Center.*) I simply won't have my vacation ruined. (*Turns.*) I live with murder all year long and it's just overdoing it to have it on my vacation. (*Picks up phone.*) Operator— Yes, this is Mrs. Hammond. Operator, I want—yes, well, thank you, Mabel, I'm sure I'll love it here, but I— Yes, I'll gladly autograph a book for you, but first will you get me the police— Yes, the sheriff— (*To* KATE.) Don't look at me like that. I tell you he's hanging in that closet. (*Into phone.*) Well, can you get in touch with him? (KATE *slowly crosses to below the closet.*) Then tell him to come right out. There's been a murder— Hello— Hello. Oh, I thought you'd fainted— Yes, murder—M-U-R-D-E-R. (*Sees* KATE *about to open closet door and screams at her.*) Don't! (*Into phone.*) No, not you, Mabel— I know I only just got here, but he got here first. Just tell the sheriff to come and get the corpse, will you, please?— Thank you. (*Hangs up.*) That girl is definitely stupid.

KATE. (*Moves Up Center.*) Are you trying to get my reaction for a story? Is that it? Because, if you are, I have no reaction other than to think you're nuts.

CRANE. Let's just forget it. There's nothing to do until the sheriff comes. Don't mention it again. (*She sits quite calmly in the Center chair.*) Mix me a drink, will you?

KATE. I certainly will not. Do you mean to sit there and have me honestly believe that a strange gentleman is hanging up in there?

CRANE. I'm not even sure he's a gentleman. Now, Kate, be sensible, you've taken dictation on enough murder stories not to be shocked. Bodies always appear in closets of houses when people move in.

KATE. Well, I'm going to see for myself.

CRANE. All right, if you have no faith in me. (*Puts fingers in her ears.*) I hate to hear people scream.

(KATE *crosses to the closet, gingerly puts her hand on the knob and opens it. It is empty. She comes back to* CRANE *and takes her fingers out of her ears.*)

KATE. How about taking a nap?

CRANE. You're behaving very calmly, I must say. You're a lot braver than I thought.

KATE. Would you like me to call a doctor, Crane?

CRANE. An undertaker. The man is dead.

KATE. There is no one in the closet.

CRANE. (*Rises and faces closet.*) Will you please look carefully in there. Kate, he's gone! (*Rushes into closet.*) It's empty. Where did he go?

KATE. Little Eva went to heaven.

CRANE. No, be serious. Someone stole him. Look, there's another door. (*She goes through the inner closet door on the Right wall.*) The closet has two doors. It's the library. (*From Offstage.*) What a wonderful collection. Oh, "Little Women." I haven't read that for years. (*KATE goes to the closet and looks in.* CRANE *comes out through the passageway to Up Center in the arch carrying a book. She comes down to* KATE, *who is peering into the closet.*) Here I am. You see, Kate, someone stole the body and took it out through the library window.

KATE. Why would anyone put a body in there in the first place and then why would anyone want to steal it?

CRANE. I'm on vacation. (*Stretches out on the sofa with her head Right and thumbs through the book.*)

KATE. Will you put down "Little Women" and be sensible?

CRANE. In my books I always show that people are wrong not to wait for the police, so I'm waiting.

KATE. (*Hangs coat from back of sofa in closet.*) You really thought you saw a man hanging—where?

CRANE. (*Preoccupied with book.*) On the third hook. He was hanging by his coat collar.

KATE. What did he look like?

CRANE. Tall, nice looking, sports jacket and slacks. And a maroon ascot at the throat.

KATE. You have a vivid imagination.

(*The DOORBELL rings.*)

CRANE. Let the sheriff in.

KATE. (*Closes closet door and goes to front door.*) A vacation is supposed to be a change. (*She opens the front door and* JENNY *bounces in in one jump.*)

JENNY. Hi.

KATE. If you're the sheriff I'm going back to New York.

JENNY. I'm Jenny.

KATE. I'm Kate. Now what?

JENNY. I'm *Jenny*.

KATE. Do you have another recording?

JENNY. I bet you're Mrs. Hammond.

KATE. You lose your bet. (*Closes door.*)

CRANE. (*Sits up.*) Oh, Jenny. Kate, that's Jenny.

KATE. (*Crosses to above desk.*) I give up. You handle it.

CRANE. (*Moves to* JENNY.) You're the maid.

JENNY. Yes'm. I'm glad one of you is sensible.

CRANE. I'm Mrs. Hammond and this is Miss Bixley, my secretary.

JENNY. I'm Jenny.

KATE. That we know.

CRANE. Kate, she comes with the rent.

KATE. (*Sits on desk chair.*) Like the indoor plumbing.

CRANE. (*Leads* JENNY *into the room.*) You pay no attention to her, Jenny. Come right in. We've only just gotten here so I'm afraid I can't show you around much.

JENNY. I worked here before, Mrs. Hammond, for Marco Redfax. You know about him, I suppose? He's dead.

CRANE. Yes, Jenny.

JENNY. (*To* KATE.) I cooked for him.

KATE. Do you have any other references?

JENNY. You didn't find no diamonds yet?

CRANE. We haven't looked. All we found was—Jenny, do you know a man in a sports coat and slacks with a maroon ascot at the throat?

JENNY. No, but I'd sure like to. (*She lets forth with a high giggle.*)

KATE. My God! She giggles!

JENNY. What time do you want dinner? I had the store deliver supplies.

CRANE. How thoughtful of you, Jenny. Isn't she thoughtful, Kate?

KATE. Or hungry.

CRANE. (*To* JENNY.) Oh, seven o'clock is fine, but first bring in some ice. I'm expecting company. Miss Seymour—

KATE. And the sheriff.

JENNY. Yes'm. (*Starts for the kitchen but turns back at the door.*) Mrs. Hammond, did you really write all those books you're supposed to?

CRANE. Yes, nine so far.

JENNY. Gee—I had such a crush on your detective, Spike Wrench, you know the hero in "Blood is for Children." I thought he was real. I wrote him a fan letter.

CRANE. Then Miss Bixley probably answered you.

JENNY. You weren't very friendly.

KATE. My typewriter gets away from me.

JENNY. Mrs. Hammond, you sure write tough.

CRANE. Thank you—I think. (*Takes a cigarette from table by chair.*)

JENNY. You sure know a lot about sex. How'd you find out?

CRANE. I read. (*Lights cigarette.*) Jenny, hadn't you better get to the kitchen?

JENNY. Yes'm. Maybe sometime we can sit down and you'll tell me how to be a femme fatal.

CRANE. Fatale.

JENNY. I don't care, just so I kill them. (*She giggles and goes into the kitchen.*)

KATE. (*Looking after her.*) Better and better. The maid is probably the taxi driver's mistress.

CRANE. (*Crosses to below sofa.*) She's a sweet, poor country child. Probably walked two miles to school through snow with her dear little feet swathed in burlap.

KATE. That was Valley Forge!

CRANE. You can be as sarcastic as you want. I love it

here and I think the people are very friendly. Now I am going to look at the upstairs and start unpacking.

KATE. Keep out of the closets.

CRANE. (*Stopping at foot of stairs.*) Very funny. I tell you there was a dead man in there. Now we have to worry about a thief as well as a murderer. (*She goes upstairs.*)

(KATE *gets up and looks at the closet. She goes over to it and is just about to open it when she is startled by* JENNY *coming in from the kitchen. She carries an ice tray straight from the refrigerator.*)

JENNY. Where you want this?

KATE. (*Crosses to below chair.*) What is it?

JENNY. Ice!

KATE. (*Patiently, smiling sweetly.*) We're having company. Don't you think it would be nice to put it in a bucket?

JENNY. O.K., it's your ice. (*Starts to exit to kitchen but swings around at the door.*) And speaking of ice, I guess you want to hear all about the diamonds, huh? Maybe Mrs. Hammond could write it in a book.

KATE. Diamonds are out this season. Atomic plans are in.

JENNY. I worked for him—that Marco Redfax. He weren't no good. He smoked cigars. That's one way you can tell.

KATE. (*As she sits in the chair.*) I hope you never work for Winston Churchill.

JENNY. (*Moves in close to* KATE *and gestures with the ice tray.*) And there was police all over the place after he died in the accident. They looked everywhere for the diamonds. And they said probably his accomplice was looking, too, and a fence and everything. Then the police took everything of Mr. Redfax's to headquarters.

KATE. Did they check the closet?

JENNY. Huh?

KATE. I just thought he might have left something hanging up.

JENNY. (*As she continues waving the ice tray,* KATE *looks at the carpet and she gets some water in the eye.*) They looked everywhere.. They was police from Boston—not just the local sheriff.

KATE. Jenny, the ice is melting on the carpet.

JENNY. Yeah—you talk so much you keep me from my work. (*And she is out in the kitchen.*)

(LILLIAN *enters through French doors. She is dressed the same except that she now carries a purse and wears gloves. She sees* KATE *and throws her arms out to her.*)

LILLIAN. Kate, how are you?

KATE. (*Rises.*) Lillian, it's time you showed up. This place is a madhouse.

LILLIAN. (*After they embrace.*) Don't you like it?

KATE. I should get overtime.

LILLIAN. What's the matter?

KATE. The real estate lady is nuts, the taxi driver is out of Farmer's Almanac, and now the maid is a young Thelma Ritter. On top of everything Crane has hallucinations.

LILLIAN. (*As she crosses Left to the desk and looks towards stairs.*) Where is she?

KATE. Upstairs looking in closets, I imagine.

CRANE. (*Comes running Downstairs. She and* LILLIAN *embrace.*) Lillian, darling.

LILLIAN. Crane, I can't believe it. You're actually here.

CRANE. You look marvelous. (KATE *fades to look out windows.*)

LILLIAN. The air agrees with me.

CRANE. I'm mad about the house. Everywhere you look there's a view. Of course, Kate isn't quite as excited.

KATE. There are so many birds. If they ever get a leader, we're undone.

CRANE. Just think of it, a whole month with nothing to do.

KATE. One week then work. There certainly won't be anything to interrupt us.

LILLIAN. (*As she sits in chair Center.*) I *was* asked up for a drink.

CRANE. Didn't Jenny bring the ice?

KATE. I'm working on it. We have discussed the problem and I am holding out for an ice bucket.

CRANE. (*Crosses above desk and to Left of it.*) It's so wonderful to just move into a place like this and have everything in it—ash trays, magazines, cards—even liquor.

LILLIAN. You're paying for it, but it's worth it. One of my customers told me about Birchville. She couldn't come this year, had to go to Europe.

KATE. Why didn't we?

CRANE. (*Moves below desk.*) Europe. All those crowds and museums. This is better—just relaxing.

KATE. I could relax very easily on the beach at Cannes. (*She sits on the sofa.*)

CRANE. You'll love it as soon as you unwind. (*Sits back on the Downstage edge of the desk.*) Lillian, how's business getting along without you?

LILLIAN. Beautifully. (*She removes her gloves and puts them in her purse.*) Seems I have less and less to do every year. I make the designs and they carry them out. What I design the wealthy will wear. Personally, I wouldn't be caught dead in half the stuff—too expensive. Tell me, Crane, have you looked all through the house?

CRANE. I adore every inch of it.

LILLIAN. You're luckier than I am. My house is smaller and there's not enough room to store things. (*She rises and crosses to the closet.*) You have such wonderful closet space. (*Starts to open door.*)

CRANE. (*Rises.*) Don't! (KATE *rises.*)

LILLIAN. Don't what?

CRANE. Stay away from there, Lillian. That closet is peculiar. Oh, you might as well know. It seems we had some trouble. (*DOORBELL rings.*) Oh, dear, I know who that is. (*BELL rings again.*)

KATE. I'm on vacation. It's Jenny's job to answer doorbells. (*Calls.*) Jenny!

JENNY. (*Offstage.*) Yes'm.

KATE. The doorbell.

JENNY. (*Offstage.*) I'm not deaf.

KATE. Are you going to answer it?

JENNY. (*Offstage.*) I'm putting ice into the bucket.

KATE. (*To* LILLIAN.) This bucolic Belvedere and I are going to come to blows.

CRANE. Never mind, *I* will do it. (*Crosses and opens front door. Has it barely open when she gives a quick scream, slams it and leans against it facing front.*)

KATE. What is it?   LILLIAN. Crane, what's
                                              the matter?

CRANE. It's him—he—the one with the maroon ascot.

KATE. Out there?

CRANE. Yes.

KATE. He's alive?

CRANE. I think so. (*Peeks through door. Closes it again.*) Very much so.

LILLIAN. What are you talking about?

KATE. Well, if it's a man let him in.

CRANE. All right. (*Opens door and the body,* LYLE ROGERS, *is there.* CRANE *speaks as a perfect hostess.*) How do you do? Haven't we met before?

LYLE. Not officially.

CRANE. Come in, won't you?

LYLE. (*Does so.*) Thank you. (CRANE *closes door.*) Hello, darling.

CRANE. (*Sees he is speaking to* LILLIAN.) Darling?

LILLIAN. Crane, I told you I had some surprises for you. This is one of them—Lyle Rogers, my husband.

CRANE. Husband!   KATE. Another?

LILLIAN. (*Crosses and puts her arm through* LYLE'S. CRANE *is to their Right.*) As of last Thursday.

CRANE. Then what were you doing in my closet?

LYLE. (*Looks to* LILLIAN.) Well, you see—

LILLIAN. (*Laughs.*) Oh, dear. The whole thing didn't work out well, did it?

LYLE. No, it didn't.

KATE. Then you were in there?

LYLE. Lil put me in.

CRANE. You hung him in my closet? (KATE, *amused, sits Down Right chair.*)

LILLIAN. Well, darling, you know how I am. Here you are moving into a strange house and I wanted to do something rather sweet. And you'd never met Lyle before so I thought what better way for an introduction? I thought it would be a huge laugh.

CRANE. My hair almost turned white.

LILLIAN. I waited and waited by the phone. I even stood on my porch waiting to hear your scream.

LYLE. She just quietly fainted so I went out through the other closet door, climbed out the library window, and ran down to the house, but you must have been coming up the back way. Of course I was hanging in there forever. I kept hearing voices but you can't distinguish words through the door. (*To* CRANE.) Am I forgiven? (LILLIAN *and* LYLE *are laughing.*)

CRANE. Well, you might as well sit down. I can't blame you for Lillian's warped sense of humor.

LILLIAN. (*She takes* LYLE *by the hand and leads him to the sofa where they sit,* LILLIAN *to the Right and* LYLE *Center.*) You didn't think it was rather cute?

CRANE. No, I didn't, but for heaven's sake—married! Tell me all about it. (*She sits in chair Center.*)

LILLIAN. While you were out on the coast doing that movie script, you didn't think I was just being idle, did you? Actually, we met in the men's room at the Stork Club.

KATE. Can I have that again?

LILLIAN. You know me, I was so busy looking at everyone's clothes, I just walked right into the wrong room. Fortunately, Lyle was coming *out* and he suggested maybe I shouldn't go in. We got to talking and well— that was that.

JENNY. (*Enters carrying a regular paint bucket.*) Here you are.

KATE. (*Crosses to* JENNY.) Jenny, that is not an ice bucket. You should put the ice in the small round chromium thing with the top.

JENNY. Can't. That's what I'm cookin' the fish casserole in. This is a bucket, ain't it?

CRANE. Never mind, Kate, it's all part of the local charm.

KATE. Thank you, Jenny. (*Gingerly takes the bucket and puts it on the floor by the bar.*)

JENNY. (*She sees* LYLE.) Oh, you found him.

CRANE. Who?

JENNY. The man with the maroon ascot-thing. She was so anxious to meet you. I would be, too.

CRANE. Thank you, Jenny. That's all.

JENNY. All righty-right. (*With a huge smile at* LYLE, *she turns and goes into the kitchen.*)

KATE. That one spells trouble.

CRANE. I can't believe it, Lil. You married again.

LILLIAN. This time for keeps. (*Takes* LYLE'S *hand.*) No one really knows yet. I mean, I haven't spread the word about.

CRANE. Kate, make some drinks, will you?

KATE. Delighted. You're a sensible man, Mr. Rogers? I mean whiskey and water, none of those silly mixtures?

LYLE. I'm sensible. (KATE *starts to make highballs for everyone.*)

CRANE. Now you take good care of Lillian. She's the best.

LYLE. I wouldn't have given up the advantages of bachelorhood for anyone else.

LILLIAN. Every designing female in New York was after him.

LYLE. Now you're embarrassing me.

CRANE. But what about Walter? I mean, you did get a divorce?

LILLIAN. In a manner of speaking—yes.

CRANE. Lillian, what do you mean?

LILLIAN. I went down to Mexico in mid-April and got one of those things the movie stars get. I don't know why I never divorced Walter before. I was too busy, I guess, and never thought someone like Lyle would come along.

CRANE. I hope you don't have to pay Walter alimony.

LILLIAN. Not quite. But I won't be able to take him off my income tax as a dependent any more. (*Laughs.*) Now he's got to get a job. (*Rises and crosses to* CRANE, *suddenly more serious.*) But, Crane, there is one rather unpleasant thing. I need your help— (*DOORBELL rings.*)

CRANE. Now what?

KATE. The sheriff.

CRANE. (*Rises and crosses to front door.*) Good heavens, I almost forgot. I phoned the sheriff to come out and pick up your body.

LILLIAN. You didn't!

CRANE. I just said I did.

LILLIAN. (*Moves up to* CRANE.) Crane, wait! No one must know Lyle and I are married. You see, Walter is going to court to have the Mexican decree set aside. I don't think he'll get away with it, but it'd ruin me if the papers got hold of it.

LYLE. You know—"Designer has two husbands," and all that sort of thing.

LILLIAN. So just keep mum about it—please? (*Crosses to above* LYLE.)

CRANE. You never do anything simply, do you? (*Opens door.* VERNON *is there.*) Mr. Cookley, what do you want?

VERNON. (*Raises his hat politely.*) Question is what do you want?

CRANE. Did I forget something? Kate, did you tip Mr. Cookley?

KATE. In good Yankee dollars.

CRANE. Then what is it, Mr. Cookley?

VERNON. (*Pulls back his vest and shows his badge.*) I'm the sheriff!

KATE. Bingo! We hit the jackpot!

CRANE. I thought you were the taxi driver.

VERNON. Am. Also dog catcher, Justice of the Peace, and sexton of the Church. You got a body here?

CRANE. Body?

VERNON. Mabel called you had a body.

CRANE. Oh, that body! (*Laughs gaily.*) Oh, Mr. Cookley, the funniest thing happened— (*Her laugh trails off as she stares at* VERNON'S *face.*)

VERNON. (*Deadly.*) Ayah.

CRANE. Come in. (VERNON *comes into the room and* CRANE *closes the door.*)

VERNON. (*Tips his hat.*) Afternoon, Miss Seymour.

LILLIAN. (*Sits on the sofa in the same place as before.*) Hello, Mr. Cookley.

VERNON. Notice anything in your garden today?

LILLIAN. I haven't looked.

VERNON. I delivered a load of manure. You'll notice it if the wind shifts. (*To* CRANE.) I also deliver manure. Folks who own her house want me to tend to their garden. Now, about this here body.

CRANE. Frankly, Mr. Cookley— (*Stalling for time.*) Oh, would you like a drink?

VERNON. Of what?

CRANE. Whiskey, gin? What else is there, Kate?

KATE. Most everything.

VERNON. Don't mind if I do.

KATE. Which?

VERNON. Just mix 'em together.

KATE. You asked for it. (*Mixes him a drink from all bottles.*)

VERNON. Can I pick up the body after the drink?

CRANE. I was just going to explain—sit down, won't you?

VERNON. Don't mind if I do. (*Sits in chair Center.*)

CRANE. You see, it's really very funny. After you left, I started to unpack and— (*From outside French doors comes the voice of* HELEN *calling, "Yoo hoo! Yoo hoo!"*)

KATE. (*Crosses to* LILLIAN *and* LYLE *and hands them their drinks. Singing.*) It's so peaceful in the country.

HELEN. (*Pops in through the doors.*) Mrs. Hammond—

(*Sees the room full of people.*) Oh, you have company. Is everything all right? Mabel said you called Sheriff Cookley here. (LYLE *rises.*)

CRANE. I was just trying to explain.

HELEN. I rushed right over. It's something about a body. A dead body?

CRANE. Everything's getting rather exaggerated. (KATE *crosses to her and hands her a drink.*) You know Miss Seymour, of course?

HELEN. Rented her the house. Hello there.

LILLIAN. Haven't seen you for days, Helen.

HELEN. Rushing about—so much business. (*Looks at* LYLE.) Well, I don't know this gentleman.

CRANE. Of course not. This is the big surprise. He's—

LILLIAN. (*Warning.*) Crane!

CRANE. He's—uh—

LILLIAN. It's *Mr.* Hammond, Crane's husband. Isn't that a surprise?

CRANE. It sure is.

KATE. I'm dumbfounded. (*Hands* VERNON *the drink she brought down with* CRANE'S. *It is a ghastly color, the addition of creme de menthe having helped.*) Here you are, Mr. Cookley.

VERNON. Thanks.

LILLIAN. Lyle, this is Helen O'Toole. She rented you both the place.

LYLE. How do you do? HELEN. Delighted to know you. I thought you were at a conference.

LYLE. Not any more. (*Shoots a confused look to* CRANE.)

CRANE. I was just telling Miss O'Toole about the writers conference you were at—the one in Chicago—you know.

LYLE. Got through sooner than expected, hopped a jet, and here I am.

HELEN. I am pleased to meet such a famous columnist. This *is* my big day. (*She settles herself in chair Down*

Right.) Tell me, Mr. Hammond, do you mind being a woman?

LYLE. (*This has caught* LYLE *just as he is about to sit. He freezes and straightens up again.*) I beg your pardon?

HELEN. Or should I call you Dorothy?

LYLE. Dorothy?

LILLIAN. The column, Lyle.

CRANE. Your lonelyhearts column—the one you write.

LYLE. (*Catches on.*) Oh, yes, of course. I make it a policy never to discuss business while on vacation. (*Sits on sofa.*)

KATE. (*Sits at the desk with her drink. Mischievously.*) Ask him a question. Get his advice. Go on.

CRANE. Some other time, Miss O'Toole. Lyle is just exhausted from his flight. Would you like a drink?

HELEN. No, thanks. Now, tell me, Mrs. Hammond, about this body. Mabel was quite excited.

CRANE. You see, it was like this—

JENNY. (*Bangs in through kitchen door.*) Dinner in five minutes!

CRANE. Thank you, Jenny. Do we have enough for company?

JENNY. Nope! (*She goes back into kitchen.*)

CRANE. (*Crosses above chair to Left of sofa.*) Sorry I can't ask you all to stay. It's been so nice having you all drop around. We must get together some other time. You've been a great help, Mr. Cookley. (*She looks at him but he is staring straight ahead with no expression on his face and an empty glass in his hand.*) Mr. Cookley. (*She looks to* KATE.)

KATE. He said mix 'em together.

CRANE. Mr. Cookley—

VERNON. (*A smile crosses his face.*) Call me Verne!

CRANE. Should you drink on duty?

VERNON. Duty! Yes—I have to pick up a body.

CRANE. Can't we all discuss it some other time?

LILLIAN. (*Rises, takes* LYLE's *glass and her own and puts them on table by sofa.*) Yes, it's after working hours.

Let's just pretend it never happened. Mr. Hammond, would you like to see me home?

LYLE. I'm all for that. (*He rises and they both start for French doors.*)

HELEN. But I want to know.

VERNON. (*Rises.*) As a police officer, I must investigate. (*He gets to the desk and puts his glass on it, having missed it the first time.*) Begin at the beginning. Mrs. Hammond. I must fact all the knows—er—know all the facts.

CRANE. Oh, dear, well, since you must. (*Puts her drink on table by Center chair.*) As I said I was just unpacking and I had to put something in the closet—oh, this is all too silly. You'll never believe it.

VERNON. Try me!

CRANE. Well, I walked over and opened the closet door and inside on a hook was this man— (*She walks over and opens closet door and there is another body hanging in exactly the same position as LYLE was hanging before. It is the body of a man dressed in a suit, an ordinary man but quite unconscious.*) hanging just like that and—

(*She has turned back front and now realizing what she has seen she drops in a dead faint. The others freeze as:*)

THE CURTAIN FALLS

ACT TWO

Time: *After dinner that same evening.*

At Rise: *The girls have changed into slightly more formal attire, summer cocktail dresses, and* Lyle *is in a dark summer suit. As the CURTAIN rises we find a moment of silence. Evidently* Jenny *is in far from a good mood. She bangs a tray of coffee cups down on the ·desk and returns to the kitchen.* Crane *is sitting in the chair Center,* Lyle *sits on the Right side of the sofa with* Lillian *to his Left, and* Kate *stands by the French doors. The room looks the same except that it is straightened up, the desk has the flower gone to the what-not shelf, the pocketbooks have been struck. After* Jenny *exits,* Kate *walks to above the sofa.*

Kate. That's the first time I've ever eaten a mackerel casserole.

Crane. Jenny said it was cheap. I think it was thoughtful. (Kate *crosses to desk chair and sits.*)

Lyle. (*To* Lillian.) Why don't you have a country gem like that? (*Lights cigarette.*)

Lillian. I'm on my honeymoon and I'm going to do my own cooking.

Crane. Lillian, you don't.

Lillian. I certainly do. It's a snap these days—presqueezed orange juice, instant oatmeal, frozen waffles, and last night's coffee. Then Lyle takes me out to dinner.

Kate. You mean there's a restaurant around here?

Lillian. There are several quaint places within forty miles.

Lyle. Quaint means the price is higher because the floor is uneven and you eat out of wooden bowls with worm holes in them.

Lillian. But they're darling and all antique furniture and china.

KATE. Give me those heavy old cups at the Automat.

CRANE. My husband and I met at the Automat. (*Rises and crosses to the what-not where she picks up a silent butler and empties ashtray Right of sofa.*) I'd been Christmas shopping and was dying for a cup of coffee. Also I was frozen. I had my arms full of bundles and I'd finally gotten the cup under the spout thing but I couldn't manage to pull down the lever. Then this lovely hand came over my shoulder and pulled it down with such strength of purpose that I knew it must belong to someone nice. (*Starts to put silent butler back.*) Besides it had a long index finger.

LILLIAN. That's a good sign?

CRANE. Uh-huh. Means all sorts of things.

LILLIAN. Lyle, stick out your index finger. (*He does right in her face.*) Good—long and straight.

CRANE. Don't forget Lyle is mine. You gave him to me this afternoon. (*Moves Up Left of the sofa.*) Do you think I ought to call Richard and tell him I just got married? (*This evokes laughter from all.*)

KATE. I bet he'd tell all the other girls. (*To* LYLE.) Crane's husband is the only female at the convention who *doesn't* take Serutan.

CRANE. Very funny. (*Crosses to French doors and looks out into the moonlight.*) Richard's doing his best and once his novel is out, then you'll all see how brilliant he is.

LYLE. You're an author, Crane; how do you figure out the second body this afternoon?

LILLIAN. Lyle, we agreed not to mention it.

CRANE. I suppose he's mixed up with the diamonds and that Marco Redfax, but I really couldn't care less. Besides the whole thing isn't anywhere near as good as I write. He wasn't even dead.

LYLE. But it was a good stiff knock on the head.

LILLIAN. I hope Verne phones when the body comes to. I want to know who it is.

KATE. It could be Jack the Ripper and Vernon wouldn't know.

CRANE. Oh, I bet he's smarter than we think. (*Crosses*

above sofa to LILLIAN.) I wish you wouldn't have told him Lyle and I were married. I mean, what are the people around here going to think?

KATE. They don't. They're too busy practicin' for the milkin' contest.

LILLIAN. The lawyers will take care of Walter right away. (*Angrily, she rises and crosses to the doors.*) Honestly, it was rotten of him. We haven't been living together for years and then trying to set aside the Mexican decree just because I wanted to marry Lyle. I suppose I could have bought him off.

KATE. Men are such rats. If only there was a choice. (*To* LYLE.) Present company excluded of course.

LYLE. Thank you.

CRANE. Life never runs smoothly, Lillian. Look at mine. (*Crosses up to closet.*) I rent a house with a closet like the luggage room at Bellevue. (*Moves down to below chair.*) In one day, I've moved into a new house, discovered two bodies, and find myself with two husbands. Don't you think we ought to tell Jenny about Lyle? I mean, she'll be here to get breakfast and—

LILLIAN. (*As she sees* JENNY *enter with a pot of coffee.*) No, Crane, no one must know!

(JENNY *stops dead still,* CRANE *faces her and gives a polite smile and laugh.* JENNY *looks at her and returns the smile and laugh and then puts the coffee on the desk by the tray.*)

KATE. (*As* LILLIAN *resits on the sofa.*) Jenny, you must never know what a good cook you are or we'll have to give you a raise.

JENNY. I was goin' to ask.

CRANE. (*Sits on chair Center.*) It comes out of your pay, Kate.

KATE. This is definitely not my day.

JENNY. (*Faces the room and leans on the desk.*) O.K., let's have a show of hands for coffee! (*Automatically the hands of the* OTHERS *go up.*)

CRANE. (*Stopping them.*) Everyone will take it.

JENNY. O.K. I wish Verne would call about the body. (*Pours coffee during the following. She does not fill the cups.*) I don't mind tellin' you, Mrs. Hammond, I ain't used to things like this—bodies hangin' in closets, diamonds hidden goodness knows where. I know you're used to it, being a mystery writer, but to me a dead body is a dead body and I don't like it.

CRANE. The body wasn't dead.

JENNY. It may be by now. I'm scared. I might be next.

KATE. (*Faces front. Quietly.*) My cup runneth over.

JENNY. This house ain't lucky. First Mr. Redfax gettin' killed and not findin' the ice—

LILLIAN. Ice?

JENNY. I read. (*Crosses to above sofa with two cups.*)

CRANE. (*To* LILLIAN.) Ice means diamonds.

JENNY. (*Hands coffee to* LILLIAN. LYLE *turns and puts his cigarettes out on table.*) Miss Seymour.

LILLIAN. Thank you.

JENNY. (*Hands coffee to* LYLE, *who doesn't see her.*) Mr. Hammond. (*Louder.*) Mr. Hammond.

KATE. (*As* LILLIAN *nudges* LYLE.) That's you—coffee?

LYLE. Oh, thanks, Jenny.

(JENNY *turns and gives* CRANE *a look, then crosses and hands cups to* CRANE. KATE *takes her own from desk.*)

CRANE. He's deaf.

JENNY. Really?

CRANE. (*Compounding the lie.*) Yes—the war, you know. Water pressure on the inner ear. He was a frogman. Fins and all that. He had to stay under for hours strapping bombs on U-Boats in the fjords. Got all kinds of ribbons, didn't you, dear?

LYLE. All kinds—blue, red, gingham.

KATE. Every night at sunset, Mrs. Hammond sings "My Hero."

JENNY. Gee, maybe you'd autograph my waterwings.

CRANE. (*Looks into her cup.*) Jenny——
JENNY. Yes'm.
CRANE. What's this?
JENNY. What?
CRANE. This half cup of coffee.
JENNY. That's what Miss Bixley wrote on the dinner menu.
KATE. I said a demi-tasse.
JENNY. And I said what's a demi-tassey and you said half a cup of coffee.
KATE. But it comes in half a cup.
JENNY. Then it's a full cup. If a cup is full, it isn't half.
KATE. Jenny, demi means half. It's French.
JENNY. Then you want half a tassey. How much is a tassey?
KATE. (*To* CRANE.) You take over.
CRANE. (*Patiently.*) Jenny, in French, tasse means cup.
JENNY. (*Exploding in anger.*) Then that's what you've got—a demi-tassey. Half a cup! What you complainin' about?
CRANE. (*Giving up.*) Nothing, Jenny.
JENNY. Out here, folks want a cup of coffee, they drink a cup of coffee. (*Starts to kitchen door.*) I think you're all demi-wits. (*She slams out.*)

(*Silence as they all drink.*)

CRANE. To top the whole thing, it's instant.
LYLE. Not only do I have two wives, but now I'm an ex-frogman and deaf to boot.
LILLIAN. (*Laughing.*) Only slightly deaf.
LYLE. You know, Crane, I think this whole thing is getting out of hand. (*Rises and crosses to* CRANE.) Suppose something gets in the papers. I mean if the police are going to be poking around here, it might do Lillian more harm than good.
CRANE. If this were one of my books, I'd start over.
LILLIAN. (*Rises and puts cup on sofa table.*) I think

we'd better be going before anything else happens. (*Holds out her hand to* LYLE *who joins her.*)

CRANE. Thanks for standing by us, you two. As soon as things straighten out, I'll get you the best present Fifth Avenue has to offer.

KATE. (*Rises and moves below desk.*) You're giving her back her husband for the night. What more does she want?

CRANE. Say, what if I need him back again? Suppose someone asks?

LYLE. Just give me a call and I'll be right up.

LILLIAN. We're only down the hill. (*Starts for doors.*)

LYLE. And let us know about the body when you find out.

CRANE. (*Crosses to them.*) Go before Jenny sees you or she'll spread the rumor we're being divorced.

LILLIAN. Good night. We'll call bright and early.

LYLE. Not too early. (LILLIAN *pulls him out through French doors.*)

KATE. There goes your husband off on his honeymoon.

CRANE. (*Waving after them.*) What Noël Coward could do with this.

KATE. He seems nice. I give Lyle my seal of approval.

CRANE. Lillian deserves some happiness.

KATE. (*After a pause.*) Now what? More instant?

CRANE. Thanks. (KATE *takes* CRANE'S *cup to desk and refills it and then her own.*)

KATE. You want me to move into the master bedroom with you tonight?

CRANE. (*Crosses to* KATE.) Of course not.

KATE. You're not scared?

CRANE. No.

KATE. Well, I am.

CRANE. (*Moves above chair with her cup.*) Kate, this has nothing to do with us. We just happened to move in at the wrong moment. Marco and his diamonds and whoever was hanging up in there are probably connected, but we're innocent bystanders.

KATE. (*Gesturing with cup.*) The passengers on the

Titanic didn't ram the iceberg but they went down with the ship.

CRANE. I'll have to think that one over.

(DOORBELL rings.)

KATE. (*With a look toward the kitchen.*) Any bets on Jenny answering? Give you two to one—three to one—five to one—

CRANE. Jenny!

JENNY. (*Offstage.*) I'm washing.

KATE. Herself or the dishes?

CRANE. (*Goes to front door.*) This is all part of rustic country charm.

KATE. Oh, for the vulgarity of a simple little suite on Sutton Place.

(CRANE *opens the door and* VERNON *is there. He wears a suit jacket over his vest and he tips his hat as usual.*)

VERNON. I'm back.

KATE. (*As she sits on desk chair.*) He must be getting overtime.

CRANE. Come in, Mr. Cookley, or may I call you Verne?

VERNON. (*As he comes into the room and* CRANE *closes the door.*) Don't see why not, it's my name.

CRANE. Coffee?

VERNON. Never touch it after breakfast.

KATE. I'm that way about whiskey.

CRANE. (*As she moves above sofa.*) We're dying to know, Verne; tell us about the body.

JENNY. (*Enters from kitchen, drying her hands on a towel.*) Oh, you answered it.

CRANE. Thank you anyway.

VERNON. (*Tips his hat.*) Evenin', Jenny. Evenin', Miss Bixley.

KATE. (*Being real folksy.*) Pull up a chair and set a spell.

VERNON. (*Sits in chair Center.*) That's right friendly of you.

KATE. It works.

VERNON. I might as well tell all of you at once. Where's Mr. Hammond?

CRANE. In Chicago—oooooooh, that Mr. Hammond. He's—

KATE. Upstairs.

CRANE. Taking a shower.

VERNON. T'ain't Saturday night.

CRANE. He loves the water.

JENNY. In the war he was a frog! (*She returns to the kitchen.*)

CRANE. (*After* VERNON *looks at her for an explanation.*) She's confused it with the fairy tale about the frog who turned into a prince. Charming little thing. (*Sits on the sofa.*) Now about the body—who was he?

VERNON. Well, after we got him back to Doc Parsons, he come to. Says his name is Philip Smith. Seemed he'd been hit on the head—

CRANE. With a blunt instrument—

VERNON. Say, you're right clever. How'd you know that?

CRANE. I always read my own books.

VERNON. It's the truth. He don't know who did it or how he got in there. Doc is bandagin' him up now. Then I'm going to take him down to the jail.

KATE. Birchville has a jail?

VERNON. It's my bathroom. We put bars on the window. Of course, I could keep an eye on him better if the jail was right *in* the house.

KATE. How quaint—an out-jail.

CRANE. Where was he hit?

VERNON. On the head.

CRANE. I mean where? Inside the house? Because if he was, what was he doing here?

VERNON. That's a very good question. I gotta ask him that sometime. (*Rises and moves toward* CRANE.) Well, I can't stay no longer. Gotta get back to Doc's, but

I wanted you to know what happened. (*Moves toward front door, but turns back.*) Say, I better have a look around before I go. You know, make sure everything is as straight as a row of corn. Want to check the closets and upstairs and all.

CRANE. (*Crosses to his Right.*) How thoughtful of you. Go right ahead.

KATE. (*Rises.*) Crane!

CRANE. Yes.

VERNON. Sure wish I could find them diamonds some-where.

CRANE. (*To* KATE.) What? (KATE *moves up to* VER-NON'S *Left and gestures franticaily up the stairs.* CRANE *looks blank.* KATE *makes a gesture of turning on some-thing.*) What are you doing?

KATE. Shh! (*Then she makes a gesture of water com-ing down over her.* CRANE *still looks blank and* KATE *gives up.*)

CRANE. (*Gets an idea.*) How many words? (KATE *holds up four fingers.*) Four. (KATE *nods, then repeats the turning gesture.*) Round? (KATE *shakes her head.*) Turn? (KATE *nods.*) Turn on something. Turn on—the— (KATE *makes water splashing gesture again.*) Rain—water— (KATE *starts washing and dancing around.*) Shower! (KATE *collapses.* CRANE *notices* VERNON *who has been fascinated. She laughs gaily.*) Games! Every night after dinner we play games. Vernon, if you'll excuse me a minute, I'll check on Mr. Hammond. (*As she goes up-stairs.*) Don't want to give him a heart attack in the shower.

VERNON. (*To* KATE.) I'm good at games, too. What's this? (*He holds his left index finger straight up behind his head and puts his nose between his right index and second finger and winks his right eye.*)

KATE. Sailor on forty-second street?

VERNON. Pontiac makin' a right turn.

KATE. Say, that's good.

JENNY. (*Enters.*) I'm most near finished now. I'll be gettin' along soon.

KATE. Don't forget the coffee cups.

JENNY. (*As she collects two cups from sofa table and one from chair table.*) If only people would have coffee at the table like they oughta. I'll be back for breakfast. What you both like?

KATE. (*Moves to above sofa.*) Just orange juice and coffee.

JENNY. And?

KATE. That's all.

JENNY. Hardly any use comin' at all.

VERNON. I always have a good hunk of meat in the mornin'. Sunday it's pork chops and sometimes a piecea pie.

KATE. (*Almost ill.*) Just juice and coffee.

CRANE. (*Comes to foot of stairs.*) You can come up now, Verne. Mr. Hammond's still in the shower, but you can check the other rooms.

VERNON. I'll feel better knowin' no one else is here. I called the police in Boston and they said there's already a private detective somewhere according to what they hear and they said some stool pigeon—is that right, Mrs. Hammond?

CRANE. Perfect.

VERNON. Some stool pigeon told them the fence is here, too.

CRANE. (*Indicating the stairs.*) Shall we? I don't want to run down the water supply.

VERNON. (*Passing* CRANE.) Oh, by the by, after I check up here, I'll put that Philip Smith in jail and then I'll come back. I wanna see Mr. Hammond. Want to be sure he can protect you case anything happens. He oughta be through his shower by then, no matter how dirty he is. (*He goes upstairs.*)

CRANE. (*Crosses to* KATE *quickly. Sotto voce.*) Kate— phone Lillian and tell her I want to borrow— (*Sees* JENNY *standing there interested.*) that thing for a few minutes.

KATE. Roger.

CRANE. Over and out. (*She runs upstairs.*)

JENNY. (*As she starts to exit with tray of cups.*) Anything I can lend Mrs. Hammond?

KATE. (*Moves to above desk.*) No, thanks, Jenny. It's something you don't have and I don't have. Dammit.

JENNY. My mother says swearing is just a lack of vocabulary. (*She exits.*)

KATE. (*Into phone.*) Operator, get me— No, this isn't Mrs. Hammond. I'm Miss Bixley, her secretary. Will you get me— Yes, I'm sure we'll love it here, Mabel. It's so peaceful. Will you get me— (*Finally she blows up.*) Do you know, in New York operators are recorded—they're robots. If I report you to the union, you'll be replaced by machinery, now get me Miss Seymour, it's an emergency! —Lillian, Kate. Quick, we're in trouble. That rustic Sherlock Holmes wants to question Crane's husband. We have him in the shower but he's got to come out sometime. So—(*Jenny caters for coffee pot.*) send that thing over, will you? Just for a little— Don't worry, we won't keep it all night. Just till things are cleared up. Bye now. (*Turns to* JENNY.) Vaporizer. I'm allergic to fresh air.

(*She runs upstairs suppressing a sneeze. After she is out of sight, the sneeze explodes.* JENNY *picks up the coffee pot and turns to the kitchen door but a loud "psst!" stops her. She freezes. Another "psst!" from the French doors and* RANDOLPH *pokes his head in.* JENNY *slowly turns.*)

JENNY. (*A smile of relief when she sees who it is.*) Oh, I thought you was a rattlesnake.

RANDOLPH. They're only out West. Is the coast clear?

JENNY. (*Puts coffee pot on Downstage edge of desk and crosses above to closet door.*) No. Everyone's upstairs, even the sheriff. And what's more, now the husband has come.

RANDOLPH. (*Crosses to her.*) When can we search?

JENNY. Later tonight. I got a key. I was just about to leave. I'll come back later and we can look for the

diamonds while they're sleepin'. I'll meet you here at
Two A.M.

RANDOLPH. O.K. (*They shake.*) I haven't even been
able to get in touch with the Boss. Every one is on the
run tonight, but I guess it don't matter. (*Moves below*
JENNY *to Up Center.*) Geez, that ice gotta be here somewhere.

JENNY. (*Opening the closet door.*) And there was a
body hung up in the closet.

RANDOLPH. Dead? (*He stands in the closet doorway.*)

JENNY. Verne said he was knocked out. I heard them
talkin'. No one knows who he is. (*From upstairs come
the voices of* CRANE, KATE, *and* VERNON.) Here they
come. Get in there. Quick! (*She pushes him in.*)

RANDOLPH. Pigeon, this ain't dignified!

(*She closes the door on him just as they come downstairs,*
CRANE *first, followed by* VERNON *and* KATE.)

CRANE. I feel so much better knowing you've checked
the house, Verne. Oh, Jenny, finished clearing up?

JENNY. I just have to wash out the coffee pot and then
I'm off. (*She picks up pot from desk.*)

CRANE. Better check here, too, Verne. This has been a
very busy closet today.

VERNON. Just as you say. (JENNY *is frozen facing
front. A small "oh" escapes from her. She closes her
eyes.*)

KATE. If you find another body, I quit.

CRANE. (*Opens the closet door. The closet is empty.*)
See? All clear. (VERNON *and* CRANE *go to the front door
as* JENNY, *amazed, heads for the closet.*) Thanks again,
Verne, and we'll see you a little later.

VERNON. (*Takes off his glasses and cleans them on his
handkerchief.* JENNY *peers inside closet. She is still carrying the coffee pot.*) Just as soon as I put that Philip Smith
in jail, I'll bring your husband a gun. He oughta have it.

KATE. I'm all shot now. (*Laughs drily.*)

CRANE. That's very sweet of you. (JENNY *has closed*

*the closet door and taken a few steps Downstage trying
to figure it out. The door opens and* RANDOLPH *gets right
behind her.* JENNY *starts walking to kitchen and* RAN-
DOLPH *walks behind her in lock step. They exit. The
others are talking and not noticing all this.*) You know,
Verne, they could make a television series out of you
rural keepers of justice. "Just Plain Verne," the story of
a man who knows no fear.

(*From the kitchen* JENNY *lets out a piercing shriek.*)

CRANE. That's Jenny.
KATE. Probably tasted the coffee.
JENNY. (*Pops out of kitchen.*) Sorry, Ma'am. I was
frightened by a mouse. I'll be leavin' now.
CRANE. Did you lock the back door?
JENNY. Yes'm, after I chased out the mouse.
VERNON. I'm goin' down past your place, Jenny. I'll
give you a lift.
JENNY. All righty-right. (*Crosses to front door.* VER-
NON *goes out.*)
VERNON. See you ladies later.
KATE. Can't wait.
CRANE. And my husband will be here, won't he, Kate?
KATE. He sure will.
JENNY. Night, everyone.

(JENNY *exits and* CRANE *closes the door and leans against
it.* KATE *staggers to chair Center and sits.*)

CRANE. Is it time for a commercial? I feel like we're
on "The Untouchables."
KATE. This sort of thing doesn't happen in the city,
you know. Just traffic, robberies, muggings, simple things
that one can cope with.
CRANE. (*Crosses to above* KATE.) You have no love
of adventure, Kate. This has been a wonderfully exciting
day.
KATE. Why didn't Lillian say Lyle was my husband?

Then I would have had Verne stand guard outside our room all night.

CRANE. (*Sits on the Left arm of the sofa.*) Say, if you want a husband, how about Vernon?

KATE. He has pork chops for breakfast.

CRANE. I don't know whether to try and write all this to Richard and Kathy or not. A daughter might understand, but a husband—never.

KATE. Kathy! I forgot. You have a letter from her—it's in the top desk drawer.

CRANE. (*Gets letter.*) I hope she's liking camp better. It's very important to have your first job a pleasant one.

KATE. This is my first. Straight from Katherine Gibbs to you. (*As CRANE scans the letter.*) Let's see, how many years has it been? (*Counts on her fingers.*) It can't be!

CRANE. Poor kid. She got poison ivy. (*Goes to bar and mixes a highball for herself and Kate.*)

KATE. I wonder how Kathy would like having two fathers.

CRANE. She'd love it, but the Camp would fire her. She loves tennis, so what do they put her in charge of? Sunday nature walks. And she's cheerleader, too. (*Hands* KATE *her drink.*) But that's Kinni-Killi-Wock-Nock.

KATE. I beg your pardon.

CRANE. Kinni-Killi-Wock-Nock. That's the name of the camp. (*Returns to bar for her drink.*) Indian and all that.

KATE. If they ever do a locomotive cheer, it'll run past taps.

CRANE. How about a murder story in a summer camp? Good gimmick. Who put the Killi in Kinni-Killi-Wock-Nock?

KATE. It'd be banned in Boston.

CRANE. (*Crosses to doors.*) I'm going to hate getting down to work next week.

KATE. If I had notes on the last two hours, you wouldn't have to.

CRANE. Do you suppose those diamonds really are

here? Verne said there was a private investigator in town, and the Boss. Want to look?

KATE. I'm game. I won the treasure hunt at our Sunday School picnic when I was fourteen.

CRANE. What was the prize?

KATE. Oh, I didn't win that, but Chet Martin and I got lost in the woods and that was prize enough for me.

CRANE. (*Moves below sofa.*) Kate, you're incorrigible.

KATE. Didn't you ever go to Sunday School?

CRANE. Of course, but I spent the whole time thinking of different ways to murder the teacher. You know, I'd make a damn good murderer. (*Sits on sofa.*)

KATE. Uh-uh. You never commit the perfect crime. You always have the murderer caught.

CRANE. All my writing career, I've wanted to have the usual party at the end—you know, where they invite all the suspects. Then I'd have the detective say, (*In a deep voice.*) "I know who the murder is." Then you'd turn the page and it'd say, (*In a cute, little girl voice.*) "Guess who?" But I don't think it would sell.

KATE. Put enough sex in any story and it'll sell. Look at "Forever Amber," "Peyton Place," "The Yearling."

CRANE. What's sexy about "The Yearling"?

KATE. (*With a wicked leer.*) A little boy who falls in love with a deer?

CRANE. (*Rises.*) Let's look for the diamonds. (*Puts her glass on the table by the Center chair.*) The trouble is as soon as we really start searching, someone will come in, won't he?

KATE. This quiet, hidden-away nook is like Macy's at Christmas.

CRANE. So the sensible thing is to wait until we're sure we won't be interrupted.

KATE. A good thought for one of your height and weight.

CRANE. But when?

KATE. (*Takes both glasses to bar.*) Later tonight when the milking is done, the quilts have been patched and the Late Show is finished.

CRANE. Pick a time.

KATE. One—two—three?

CRANE. Two sounds safe enough.

KATE. It's a deal. Two A.M. and we ransack the joint. (*They shake hands.*)

CRANE. Didn't I have one of these scenes in "The Case of the Bloody but Unbowed Head"?

KATE. Sure you did.

CRANE. That's right. They spent the night looking for the stolen money and in the morning they were found all walled up with a cask of Amontillado.

KATE. You're confusing yourself with Poe. (*PHONE rings.*) You take it. I can't face Mabel again.

CRANE. (*Crossing to phone below* KATE.) Hel'o - Oh, yes. (*To* KATE.) You're clairvoyant. (*In phone.*) I'm sorry, Mabel, but Sheriff Cookley left a few minutes ago. He took Jenny home. Maybe you can catch him there. Is it anything serious?—In that case I wouldn't think of letting you tell me. (*Hangs up.*) It seems telephone operators take an oath like doctors. They can't reveal secrets.

KATE. Maybe they've caught someone.

CRANE. Who?

KATE. Oh, anyone. The Boss, the fence, the private operator.

CRANE. Maybe Verne's term of office has expired.

KATE. Another drink? (*Crosses to bar and makes two drinks.*)

CRANE. We need fortitude for the search.

KATE. I'll never sleep a wink anyway.

CRANE. Why not?

KATE. Listen. Could you sleep with all that going on? Just listen. (*Cups hand to ear.*) Not a damn thing. Oh, for one car or one good street brawl.

CRANE. (*Crosses above sofa to doors.*) The country is full of the most fascinating sounds, Kate. You're just not attuned to them—little crickets rubbing their legs together, owls hooting at the moon, little bobolinks linking.

KATE. (*Moves to above sofa with* CRANE'S *drink.*) I don't hear a damn thing.

CRANE. (*Meeting* KATE *above sofa, both facing front.*) Concentrate. Listen to nature, Kate. It's magnificent. (*After a slight pause comes the sound of* HELEN's "Yoo Hoo.")

KATE. (*Handing* CRANE *her drink.*) The Audubon Society should get that one.

HELEN. (*Offstage.*) Yoo hoo. (*And in she bounces dressed as before.*) Guess who?

KATE. Would you repeat the question, please?

HELEN. Guess *who?*

CRANE. Why, Miss O'Toole, what a pleasant surprise. I was just saying I bet someone would drop in.

KATE. And here you are. Would you like a drink?

HELEN. No, thank you. Mrs. Hammond, I feel awful.

CRANE. Kate, get an aspirin.

HELEN. I don't mean physically. I mean I feel awful about what's happened to you today. (KATE *goes to the bar for her drink.*)

CRANE. Nothing at all has happened to me. (*Puts her glass on table by chair.*)

HELEN. (*Moves in below sofa.*) Here you move in all exhausted from your writing and what happens? Bodies hanging in closets, police in and out, missing diamonds. You mustn't think Birchville a very friendly place.

CRANE. On the contrary. (*Indicates for* HELEN *to sit on sofa, which she does, placing her purse on the table to the Right.* CRANE *sits beside her.*)

HELEN. As a matter of fact, I brought this very matter up at the Maple Products committee meeting tonight. To make amends, we'd like you to accept the honor of being our Sap Queen.

CRANE. Sap Queen?

KATE. Don't question it. (*Sits in Center chair.*)

HELEN. Yes. Every spring when the syrup is running, we always have an honorary Sap Queen at the square dance. Even if you can't be here in person, it doesn't matter. We'll put your picture on every can of sap that is made in town. That's how we feel about you, Mrs. Hammond.

CRANE. I'm deeply touched, really I am. Isn't it sweet, Kate?

KATE. Sweet—and sticky.

HELEN. Last year's Sap Queen was a great disappointment. She ran off with a married man and the committee had to spend the summer pasting another face over hers on the can.

KATE. Who did they pick?

HELEN. What could they do? It was an emergency. They just glued on Mary Pickford and hoped for the best.

CRANE. I hope you won't have to glue anyone over me.

HELEN. Have no fear, I know a lady when I meet one. You're not the type to run away with a married man.

CRANE. No, I'd stay home with him, wouldn't I, Kate?

KATE. Only with your best friend's husband.

(*They* BOTH *laugh.* HELEN, *not understanding joins them, turns toward doors to pick up her purse, sees something outside, screams and rises, pointing out doors. The* OTHER TWO *rise also.*)

CRANE. What is it?   KATE. Miss O'Toole!

HELEN. Out there. I saw him.

CRANE. Who?

HELEN. A man. I'm sure of it. A prowler.

KATE. In our garden?

HELEN. Yes. I just caught a glimpse of him but I think he was wearing pajamas. (HELEN *looks out doors,* CRANE *and* KATE *face each other and make turning gesture and water-coming-down gesture.*)

CRANE. It's just your mind playing tricks. Auto-suggestion and all that sort of thing.

HELEN. I saw him!

CRANE. (*As she sits* HELEN *on the sofa and sits beside her.*) You think you saw him, that's all. You're just nervous because of all that's happened. Isn't that right, Kate? (KATE *nods and moves above them. To* HELEN.) Miss Bixley majored in psychology in Princeton.

HELEN. Princeton?

KATE. It was a correspondence course.

HELEN. I would have sworn I saw a man out there in his pajamas.

KATE. I understand. We old maids all get that way.

HELEN. I didn't mean anything like that, Miss Bixley. (*DOORBELL rings.* CRANE *and* KATE *freeze looking at each other.* HELEN *looks at each of them. DOORBELL rings again.*) I suppose I'm imagining that bell.

CRANE. I hope it isn't the pajamas.

KATE. So do I.

HELEN. It can't be. They're imaginary.

CRANE. (*Crosses to the door as* KATE *pats* HELEN *reassuringly. Opens door and* VERNON *is there.*) Oh, Vernon, back so soon?

VERNON. Got a phone call from Doc Parsons—evenin', Miss Bixley. Helen. (*He tips his hat.*)

HELEN. Hello, Verne.

VERNON. (*Comes into room and Right of arch.*) Seems that Philip Smith escaped from the Doc's office.

HELEN. Was he wearing pajamas?

VERNON. Nope. Suit. I thought I better high-tail it up here case he tried to get back in. (*Pulls out pistol.*) Brought this for your husband. He might need it.

CRANE. (*Takes it.*) Thanks. I'll see he gets it.

VERNON. (*Takes pistol back.*) Nope. Gotta show him how it works. If he can't handle firearms, you might get shot.

CRANE. He was here just a moment ago, wasn't he, Kate?

KATE. (*With a glance out the doors.*) The littlest moment ago.

CRANE. I'll go upstairs. He's probably writing his column. I hate to disturb him when he's working. You absolutely have to see him?

VERNON. Absolutely.

CRANE. All right. Kate, come and help me in case he gets violent. I think I'll need some help.

KATE. I'm sure you will. (*They both rush upstairs.*)

VERNON. (*Crosses Down to* HELEN.) Funniest pair of females.

HELEN. I think she's delightful –Mrs. Hammond. The other one is peculiar.

VERNON. (*Sits next to* HELEN.) How do you know she's Mrs. Hammond—*the* Crane Hammond?

HELEN. She told me.

VERNON. Ayah.

HELEN. And her friend, Miss Seymour, said so.

VERNON. How you know those two females ain't workin' in cahoots with that Seymour? They might all be fences.

HELEN. I never thought of that.

VERNON. Or one of 'em might be the private detective who's come up here. They might find the diamonds and scoot off with 'em.

HELEN. (*Rises.*) Of course. Vernon, you're a regular Sherlock Holmes.

VERNON. Then again, they might be just nice folks.

HELEN. I have a suggestion. (*She rushes up to the foot of the stairs, glances up them and then signals* VERNON *to join her. Sotto voce.*) They're tired after their travels so why don't we come back here later and have a look for the jewels? Just the two of us.

VERNON. Tonight, eh?

HELEN. When they're asleep.

VERNON. You birthed an idea, Helen. We'll do it. What time?

HELEN. Midnight?

VERNON. Too early. They're city folks. They'll be drinkin'. Make it two o'clock.

HELEN. All right. We'll meet here at Two A.M. (*They shake on it.*)

VERNON. How're we goin' to get in? You got an extry key?

HELEN. No. I gave one to Jenny and the other to Mrs. Hammond. Let's unlock the back door?

VERNON. You got a right good thought for a real estate lady. You go on like this and I'll make you a deputy.

HELEN. Come on. We'd better hurry. (*They both trot out the kitchen door. As the door swings shut,* LYLE *enters through French doors. He is dressed in pajamas, robe, slippers, and an ascot. He crosses to the stairs, looks up them, comes back into the room and is below the closet door as* HELEN *and* VERNON *come in.* LYLE *pops into the closet.*) I hope they don't lock it again.

VERNON. They think it's locked already.

CRANE. (*Offstage.*) All right, darling. I'll try to explain.

HELEN. They're comin' back. Look casual. (*They both bolt across the room.* HELEN *ends up in chair Down Right and* VERNON *sitting dead front on the sofa with a grin on his face.*)

CRANE. (*Comes downstairs followed by* KATE.) Really, I don't know how to apologize for Richard, Verne. (VERNON *rises.*) He's right in the middle of a dreadful problem, a letter from a girl in trouble.

VERNON. Won't the man marry her?

KATE. Not that kind of trouble. Mr. Cookley, I am shocked at you.

CRANE. So he asked me to please bring the pistol up to him. You will forgive him, won't you? Writers, you know.

KATE. They're such a stinking breed.

CRANE. Don't overdo it.

VERNON. (*Crosses towards* HELEN.) I don't know if I should.

CRANE. Besides, we'll be quite safe. The kitchen is locked already. I'll lock the front door and the French doors. See—no one in the closet. (*She opens the closet door and* LYLE *is standing there. She gives a quick scream, slams the door and leans against it. No one else in the room has seen* LYLE.)

HELEN. (*Rises.*) What is it?

CRANE. Nothing. Nothing at all. (*Holds her knee.*) An old war injury.

VERNON. You in the war?

KATE. Gang war! (*Slowly moves in to* VERNON.) When

she was just a kid on the East Side. But she worked her way out of poverty to what she is today—a shining example to all those poor unfortunates. (*Faces front dramatically.*) Yes, Mr. Cookley, America is a land of opportunity!

CRANE. Are you going to sing "God Bless America"? She has a lovely voice. If you'll just excuse me a minute. I want to get a book. Always read myself to sleep. (*She whizzes out to the library through the Up Center passageway.*)

KATE. (*Moves Up following* CRANE.) That's one thing I'll say for Crane. She reads other people's books.

HELEN. (*Moves to* KATE.) She seems mighty upset this evening. Is she always this way?

KATE. (*Crosses to* VERNON.) Not at all. She's calm as a cucumber.

VERNON. Cool.

KATE. I beg your pardon.

VERNON. Cool as a cucumber.

KATE. (*Crosses below* VERNON *to his Right.*) Isn't it calm? (*Turns on him.*) How can a cucumber be cool sitting in the sun all day?

VERNON. Never thought of it that way.

HELEN. I hope Mrs. Hammond is emotionally stable. I mean a nervous breakdown could ruin the entire sap festival.

(*During the above dialogue,* CRANE *has led* LYLE *out Up Center and pushed him up the stairs. Now she pretends to be coming out of the library as he comes downstairs.*)

CRANE. Richard, darling, there you are.

LYLE. (*Bewildered.*) Here I am.

KATE. It's a miracle!

VERNON. Got the girl out of trouble?

LYLE. (*Looks to* CRANE, *thinking* VERNON *knows everything.*) Then you know?

KATE. No. He means the girl in your column.

LYLE. Oh, that girl. Yes, she's out of trouble but there are lots more who are in it, I'm afraid.

HELEN. We frail creatures.

VERNON. (*Crosses to* LYLE.) You know how to fire a revolver, Mr. Hammond?

LYLE. Oh, yes, I was on the team at Villanova.

VERNON. That's all I wanted to know. Don't trust females with these things, you know.

LYLE. And a very wise man you are, Mr. Cookley. (*Takes gun.*)

VERNON. That last body just escaped and he's prowling around somewhere so I want you to have protection.

LYLE. (*Moves to Left of desk examining gun.*) I'll guard the ladies with my life.

VERNON. You want a lift home, Helen? (*Moves to front door.*)

HELEN. Thanks, Verne. I'm afraid being out alone with people hiding behind every bush. I should have brought my car but with the moon out and all, I walked to the meeting.

KATE. (*Takes* HELEN'S *purse from sofa table and brings it to her.*) You country women are brave.

HELEN. (*Takes purse. Dramatically, with a smile.*) We gotta be!

VERNON. Bye again, everyone. Hope you have a peaceful night.

CRANE. I'm sure we will.

HELEN. (*As* VERNON *exits.*) Thanks again, Mrs. Hammond. I'll feel a sense of pride when I see your face on every can of sap. (*She exits.*)

KATE. (*As* CRANE *closes the door.*) Just don't ask for explanations. Its all too complicated.

CRANE. I'm glad you made it, Lyle. We had you in the shower so long, you'd have gone down the drain.

LYLE. Now what? (*Gestures with the revolver.*) Do I protect you or my lonely wife down the hill?

CRANE. (*Crosses to* LYLE *and leaves the book she got in the library on the desk.*) Don't wave that about. (LYLE *puts it in desk drawer.*) I tell you what, you go get

Lillian and come back here at two o'clock. (*She takes him to French doors by the hand.*) We're having a little search party for the diamonds.

LYLE. You really expect to find them? (KATE *moves in to Up Center.*)

CRANE. We're going to look.

LYLE. O.K. Do we share the profits?

CRANE. If there's a reward, we can split. Don't forget —two o'clock. (*Gets book on desk.*) I'm going to try to get a nap first or at least read something bright and gay.

LYLE. You're sure you don't mind being here alone?

KATE. (*With a leer.*) Any suggestions?

CRANE. Run along, Lyle, we'll be all right.

LYLE. I'll wait till you're upstairs.

CRANE. Thanks, Lyle, and once again let me say Lillian got a good man when she got you. (*Starts for stairs.*)

KATE. I agree, of course, but then I'm so desperate, any man is a good man. (*Goes upstairs.*)

CRANE. Tell Lillian I can't thank her enough for finding this secluded little retreat. Next summer I'll try Alcatraz.

(*She goes upstairs.* LYLE *looks around and then starts for French doors. As he reaches them,* VERNON *pops in.*)

VERNON. Goin' somewhere, Mr. Hammond?

LYLE. Taking an evening walk.

VERNON. Like that?

LYLE. Just a few steps. You know— (*Does a deep knee bend.*) like to feel this good country air.

VERNON. I'm takin' a final check around the house. (*As he closes doors.*) Night, Mr. Hammond.

LYLE. Night, Mr. Cookley.

(*Crosses back to the stairs and looks up them. Stands Center. Goes to bar and takes a swallow from the Scotch bottle. Crosses to doors, looks out them, sees the coast is clear, says "Gone," and exits, closing the doors. On the word cue, "Gone,"* PHILIP SMITH *stumbles in through the front door. He now wears a small gauze bandage around his head. He closes the door and leans against it.)*

PHILIP. (*His hand to his bandaged head.*) Where am I? (*Comes into the room, looks around, spies the Scotch bottle and takes a swallow from it. Crosses to Center.* CRANE *is heard humming Offstage.* PHILIP *looks for a place to hide and pops into the closet just as* CRANE *comes downstairs carrying her book. She looks at the title.*)

CRANE. "War and Peace." This will never do. (*She goes into the library.* PHILIP *comes out of the closet and closes the door. After a moment,* CRANE *comes out of the closet from the library.* PHILIP *is smashed against the wall behind the door.* CRANE *carries another book. She closes the closet door not seeing* PHILIP, *goes to the phone at the desk. Into phone.*) Mabel! Oh, do you work nights, too?—Yes, a lovely evening. Mabel, I'd like to place a long-distance call. All right, I'll hang on—

(PHILIP *starts for front door but as he hears* KATE *approach he retreats to his position by closet.*)

KATE. (*Comes downstairs and during following undoes her earrings and necklace.*) Crane, I wanted to remind you to call Richard—oh, you're doing it.

CRANE. I appreciate your efficiency anyhow.

KATE. And don't forget Kathy. You wanted—

CRANE. (*Into phone.*) Long distance? I'd like to call Chicago, Illinois. (KATE, *seeing everything is under control goes upstairs.* CRANE, *facing front does not see this.*) My number is— (*Looks at number on phone.*) 3. I guess that's all—just three. Could that be possible?—Yes, Drake Hotel. I don't know the number. Person to person to Mr. Richard Hammond— (*With a wave over towards* PHILIP'S *direction.*) Kate, pour me a brandy, will you? I'll never live through this night without it. (*She leafs through the book.* PHILIP *sneaks to look into arch and realizes* KATE *is gone. Not knowing what to do he goes above* CRANE *to bar and pours her a brandy.*) The circuits to Chicago are busy? All of them? Then let's try Miss Kathy Hammond at Camp Kinni-Killi-Wock-Nock, Meadowville, Maine. (PHILIP *hands her the brandy, first tapping her shoulder.*) No, Kinni-Killi-Wock-Nock. How do I know? It's Indian. (PHILIP *tip-toes to the front door and exits, quietly closing the door behind him.*) Those circuits are busy, too? Marooned, aren't we? Thanks anyway. (*Hangs up, takes a sip of the brandy and starts for the stairs.* KATE *comes down them carrying an empty hot water bottle. As they pass.*) Hi, Kate. (KATE *waves the hot water bottle and exits into the kitchen. Does a take.*) Kate! (*Looks after* KATE, *looks up the stairs, looks at the bar, then at the brandy. She gulps the brandy and freezes as:*)

THE CURTAIN FALLS

ACT THREE

TIME: *Two that morning.*

AT RISE: *The CURTAIN rises on a dark Stage. During
the following dark scenes, it is advisable at times
to leave a small amount of blue lights showing on
Stage. This will be indicated by the word "Blues."
At other times there must be complete blackouts.
The MOONLIGHT is flooding in through the
French doors at the moment. Everything is quiet
except for a CLOCK chiming twice. After a moment,
PHILIP comes up to the French doors, tries them
but they are bolted from the inside. The kitchen
door opens and JENNY enters carrying a flashlight. It
shakes in her hands. PHILIP immediately disappears.
JENNY glances around the room and whispers back
into the kitchen "O.K." RANDOLPH enters behind
her. He wears a handkerchief tied over his face.*

RANDOLPH. Keep your flashlight on the ground.
JENNY. It keeps shaking.
RANDOLPH. Why?
JE.INY. I'm scared.
RANDOLPH. I'll protect you.
JENNY. I'm scared of you.
RANDOLPH. Pigeon, I wouldn't hurt a fly.
JENNY. I'm scared of everything in the dark. (*For the
first time, she turns her flashlight on* RANDOLPH *and sees
the handkerchief around his face. She screams.*) What
have you got on?
RANDOLPH. A handkerchief.
JENNY. (*Switches on the DESK LAMP, which brings
up an area of light on the desk and spilling through the
Center chair so that the Left half of the room is lit.*)
What's it for?
RANDOLPH. I'm supposed to wear it.

JENNY. Why?

RANDOLPH. So no one will recognize me. This is illegal. It says right here in my instruction book, and I quote, (*He takes a small manual from his pocket.*) "It is against the law to break and enter."

JENNY. But we didn't break and enter. We just entered. I had the back door key.

RANDOLPH. That's right. We didn't break.

JENNY. So take it off.

RANDOLPH. O.K. (*He does and puts it in his pocket.*)

JENNY. That's better.

RANDOLPH. (*Crosses below* JENNY *to Center.*) Come on, we gotta start searching.

JENNY. (*Grabs his arm to stop him.*) I'm scared. I wish I'd never come.

RANDOLPH. Go on search.

JENNY. (*Loud.*) Where?

RANDOLPH. (*Puts his hand over her mouth.*) Shh!

JENNY. (*Quieting down.*) I only came 'cause you said you liked me. And now you're mean. I don't think you like me at all. I'm just a tool. I'm going home— (*She ends in a wail.*)

RANDOLPH. Pigeon— (*Puts his hand over her mouth again.*) you gotta be quiet. (*After* JENNY *subsides, he removes his hand.*) It says right here under accomplices, and again I quote, "Accomplices must be noble, loyal, trustworthy, and obedient. If a woman, promise her anything but give her Arpege." Oh, no, that's an advertisement. "Continued on Page 34." (*Finds Page* 34.) "An accomplice is a person who assists but do not trust him. No one is your friend." I don't think that, Pigeon. Once we find the jewels, I'm going to take you away from all this to somewhere exciting like Rochester.

JENNY. O.K., but you don't really trust me.

RANDOLPH. I do.

JENNY. Shouldn't I have a contract or something?

RANDOLPH. Where you get these notions?

JENNY. From Screen Star Magazine. I should get a

contract. The movie stars do. Why, I don't even know who I'm working for.

RANDOLPH. (*Crosses above desk to telephone and* JENNY *follows to his Right.*) All right, just to show you my heart's in the right place, I'll call the Boss and you can speak personal. That's how much I trust ya. (*Into phone.*) Get me— (*Covers the mouthpiece and turns away from* JENNY *as he mumbles the number.*) Huh?— My what? My call to Kinni-Killi-Wock-Nock? I don't care if the circuits are busy—You keep trying by all means. How about my number here?—O.K., bye. (*Hangs up.*) The Boss is out. Look—you search over there and I'll start over here. (*Looks in book.*) It says under places to hide jewels—"In cushions of sofas and chairs. Behind pictures. In vases."

JENNY. I looked in all them places already today. Hey, maybe they're not here at all. Maybe they're outside.

RANDOLPH. Pigeon, you are a genius. You look outside and I'll look inside. (JENNY *starts for the doors and* RANDOLPH *for the kitchen.*) I'll start in the kitchen in the icebox.

JENNY. The icebox?

RANDOLPH. Ain't you never heard of hollowed-out lettuce?

JENNY. O.K., but let me know if you find them diamonds. (*She goes out through French doors, unlocking them as she goes.*)

RANDOLPH. (*Glances in book.*) "Trust no one—not even your own mother." Silly, she was a wonderful mother. She wouldn't even get my baby food at the A & P —always shop-lifted at S. S. Pierce's. (*Puts out DESK LIGHT and goes into kitchen.*)

(*The moment the kitchen door closes, we see a FLASH-LIGHT outside the French doors. The doors open and* HELEN *enters carrying the flashlight. She crosses below the sofa and calls "Verne." Moves Up Center, turns around and calls again, "Verne." She exits by the front door unlocking it first. As soon as the front door closes,* JENNY *enters through French doors with her flashlight on. She goes immediately and noiselessly to the phone.)*

JENNY. Mabel—this is Jenny. Say, someone just called from here— Yeah, a number in town. What number was it?—17. Thanks, Mabel— Or what? 10½—what kind of a number is that?—Your shoe size! Thanks anyway, Mabel. (*Hangs up and goes out front door. The moment the front door closes,* PHILIP *comes in through French doors, leaving them open. He goes to the desk and puts on the DESK LIGHT. He looks through papers in drawers. He looks at the phone and gets an idea.)*

PHILIP. (*Into phone.*) Operator, I—you're ready with what call?—Well, yes, put it through— Who's it to again? — Kinni-Killi-Wock-Nock? Sure, why not? — Hello, Miss Wock-Nock— I beg your pardon— Oh, a camp. A summer camp. (*During this phone speech the MOONLIGHT and the BLUES fade out, leaving only the DESK LIGHT on.*) Yes, I put through the call— You see, our operators are rather stupid. Just for fun, who did she say was calling?—Mrs. Hammond— What?—Yes, I am Mr. Hammond. I guess— My daughter?—Yes, sweet thing— Her night off? Well, then never mind. Good night, Miss—oh, Chief Grogmier. Well— (*Makes Indian gesture.*) Chief, how-how! (*He hangs up.*) Hammond? Hammond? It doesn't sound like me. (*Picks up bright silver ashtray from desk and looks at his reflection.*) It doesn't look like me. Hammond! Hammond! Oh, who am I? (*He hears FOOTSTEPS from the kitchen and quickly puts out the DESK LIGHT, making it a complete BLACKOUT. The kitchen door opens.*)

RANDOLPH. Jenny, is that you?

PHILIP. (*In a high squeak.*) Ummhmmmm!

RANDOLPH. Don't make so much noise. I thought you were outside..

PHILIP. Ummmhmmmmmm!

RANDOLPH. Well, get goin'. First, I'll give you a little kiss.

PHILIP. (*In his natural deep voice.*) Uh-uh!

RANDOLPH. Come on, just a little one. (*We hear the sounds of a violent struggle.*) Say, you're strong. (*Sound of a loud slap.*) Oww! Hey, what's got into ya? Where's a light? (*He lights a match and we see he is lying over the desk.* PHILIP *has escaped to the kitchen during the above after the slap.*) Jenny. Jenny. Dames like this ain't mentioned in the instruction book.

(*The front door starts to open slowly and we see a FLASHLIGHT through it. We hear* HELEN *calling "Verne. Verne."*)

RANDOLPH. Cripes! (*He rushes out through the kitchen door.*)

HELEN. Verne, is that you? Verne, it's Helen. (*She closes the front door and comes into the room. As she is below the closet door, she sees a FLASHLIGHT outside the windows. She pops into the closet.*)

(VERNON *comes in from French doors and crosses above sofa. He carries a flashlight. As he pauses below closet door,* HELEN *opens it and when she is directly behind him, he starts moving towards kitchen door.* HELEN *leaves closet door open and walks in lock-step behind him. The only light is from the two FLASHLIGHTS. As* VERNON *is below the desk,* HELEN *whispers "Verne." He gives a surprised squeal and turns.*)

VERNON. Helen!

HELEN. Shh!

VERNON. (*For the rest of the scene, the only light is from the two FLASHLIGHTS which they hold lighting each other's face.*) You shouldn't frighten people like that. My sister was scared by a porcupine and to this day her baby's hair stands straight as a quill.

HELEN. I thought you lawmen weren't nervous.

VERNON. Good thing I didn't draw on you. I'm pretty nasty with a pistol.

HELEN. Have you found out anything?

VERNON. Nothing since I left you. 'Cept that fella that was found in the closet. Doc Parsons said when he come to he didn't know where he was or who he was. You can get that from a hit on the head, ya know—claustrophobia.

HELEN. No—that's what you get in a closet.

VERNON. He was hit in the library.

HELEN. Never mind. Let's find the diamonds. Where shall I start looking?

VERNON. Don't know.

HELEN. Then why are we here?

VERNON. Use your woman's intuition. Where would you put them?

HELEN. I see—recreate the crime and all that?

VERNON. That's right. Now you recreate while I check with Mabel, see if any more calls come through from Boston. (*Puts on the DESK LIGHT. The BLUES come on with it.*)

HELEN. All right, but don't talk too loud. (HELEN *puts on her flashlight and examines the closet, closing the door after she comes out, and along the drapes by the doors.*)

VERNON. (*Into phone.*) Mabel—this here is Verne. Verne. I can't speak up. I'm on a dangerous mission. You don't know I'm here. No one knows 'cept one person and she's with me— I ain't sayin' who— Any calls come for me?—Well, I'll check with you later--- Did I what? (HELEN *turns and moves in below sofa.*) I don't know any Kinni-Killi-Wock-Nock. Sounds like a hog at matin' time. Maybe it's code. Someone was callin' that, huh?— Thanks a lot, Mabel. Say hello to your ma. (*Hangs up.*) Helen, what's it mean—Kinni-Killi-Wock-Nock?

HELEN. Sounds Indian.

VERNON. (*Moves Up Center.*) It's a clue at any rate. That Hammond woman placed a call to Maine and that was the address. Or so she said. I don't trust her.

HELEN. (*Moves to him.*) I don't trust anyone since this whole thing started.

(Upstairs LIGHT goes on. It floods down the stairs. Sounds of KNOCKING are heard.)

CRANE. (*Offstage.*) Kate, are you asleep? It's two o'clock.

VERNON. (*Speaking during above speech.*) We gotta hide. Might catch her with the jewels. (*He darts over and puts out the DESK LIGIIT so only the BLUES remain on.*)

CRANE. (*Offstage.*) Kate! Oh, well—

HELEN. (*During above.*) Where?

VERNON. (*Opens closet door.*) In here. (*Pushes her in closet ahcad of him.*)

HELEN. Together?

VERNON. Of course.

HELEN. Can I trust you?

VERNON. (*They are standing side by side facing front;* VERNON *has his right hand on the doorknob.*) Helen, I'm the sheriff! (*Closes the door.*)

*(*CRANE *comes down the stairs immediately and puts on the ROOM LIGHTS by the switch at the foot of the stairs. She carries the book from the previous act. Mumbles, "This will never do," and goes out the passageway to the library. Immediately, the closet door opens and* VERNON *tiptoes out, followed by* HELEN. *She leaves the closet door open. They go through the passage into the library as* CRANE *comes through closet and closes the door behind her. She carries a copy of "The Raven." She starts upstairs, puts the LIGHTS out. The room is in complete BLACKOUT. She says, "Oh, Kathy, I almost forgot," and goes to the desk lamp. DESK LAMP on. Everyone is half out of hiding. They are all caught in the sudden illumination and freeze for an instant.* VERNON *is half in from the library,* HELEN *from the closet,* RANDOLPH *from the kitchen,* JENNY *from the front door, and* PHILIP *from the French doors. They*

quickly tip-toe out. CRANE, *sensing something, slowly turns just in time to miss everyone. She shrugs her shoulder and picks up the phone.)*

CRANE. (*Into phone.*) Mabel, this is Mrs. Hammond. Are the circuits clear to Maine yet?—No, I didn't get the call. (*During this conversation, the MOONLIGHT comes up outside windows.*) Never mind, it's too late now. How about the circuits to Chicago?—You did what?— Well, why did you cancel it?—Of course my husband isn't here. He's in Chicago. That's who I'm trying to call— Who?—Vernon Cookley isn't here. Do you think I'd entertain a man at this hour?—Thank you, Mabel, I don't know what you'll be quiet about but thank you. (*Hangs up.*) I'll never object to dialing again. (*Glances at the book in her hand and is delighted.*) Oh, "The Raven." (*She curls up in chair Center and reads.*)
"Once upon a midnight dreary, while I pondered, weak
        and weary
    Over many a quaint and curious volume of forgotten
        lore—"

(VERNON *tip-toes out from the library, sees her and goes
        back in again.*)

"While I nodded, nearly napping, suddenly there came a
        tapping
    As of someone gently rapping, rapping at my chamber
        door—"

(RANDOLPH *comes in from kitchen, sees her and backs
        out the swinging door.*)

"Only this and nothing more.

    Ah, distinctly I remember it was in the bleak Decem-
        ber;
    And each dying ember wrought its ghost upon the
        floor."

(HELEN *comes in from closet, sees* CRANE, *and slowly backs into closet.*)

"Eagerly I wished the morrow;—vainly I had sought to borrow
From my books surcease of sorrow—sorrow for the lost Lenore—"

(JENNY *comes in from front door, sees* CRANE *and backs out again.*)

"Nameless here forever more.

And the silken, sad, uncertain rustling of each purple curtain
Thrilled me, filled me with fantastic terrors never felt before;"

(PHILIP *comes in from windows, starts above sofa, sees* CRANE, *turns and slowly tip-toes out again.*)

"So that now, to still the beating of my heart, I stood repeating
"Tis some visitor entreating entrance at my chamber door;—
This it is and nothing more."

(*Rises and goes into the library.*) There must be something in there besides Poe. (*Re-enters with "The White Cliffs."*) "The White Cliffs." That's better. (*As she crosses to desk.*) I'm so popular. Stood up by everyone! (*Puts DESK LIGHT out.*) Oh, the moon's come out.

(*Crosses to table Right of sofa, lights a cigarette and stands there gazing out at the moonlight.* VERNON *comes out of library, starts for windows, sees her, and tip-toes upstairs. Then* RANDOLPH *comes out of kitchen, sees her and tip-toes into library.* HELEN *comes out of closet, quietly closes the door, sees* CRANE, *and tip-toes out to kitchen.* JENNY *comes in front door, closes it, sees* CRANE *and goes into closet,*

closing door after her. CRANE *walks to the Downstage side of French doors and* PHILIP *comes in
above her and tip-toes to below the stairs and hides
there.* CRANE *sighs, crosses to the stairs and goes up
reading the beginning of "The White Cliffs." Only
the MOONLIGHT and BLUES are on now.* HELEN
*comes in from kitchen with her FLASHLIGHT on.
She calls, "Verne. Verne." She crosses Up Center and
turns, surveying the room.* PHILIP *comes from below
the stairs and puts his hand over her mouth and
drags her out the front door, closing it after him.)*

JENNY. (*Comes out of the closet, her flashlight on.*)
Randolph! Randolph!

RANDOLPH. (*Comes from library and down to* JENNY.)
I'm here, pigeon, but so is everyone else. It's like the
Olympic Games. Someone almost came into the library.
I hid behind the drapes.

JENNY. I'm scared. I think I'm gonna cry again.

RANDOLPH. (*Takes her flashlight and puts it on table
by chair.*) Now, now, Jenny, pigeon.

JENNY. I feel it comin'. I'm gonna let go.

RANDOLPH. Come on, let it go outside. (JENNY *sniffles
and* RANDOLPH *starts to lead her out windows.*) The
flashlight! (JENNY *continues out and he goes back for
flashlight. As he picks it up.*) Ah!

(*As he starts out again, there is a bloodcurdling scream
from* KATE *upstairs.* RANDOLPH *pops into the closet.
LIGHT goes on upstairs.)*

CRANE. (*Offstage.*) Kate—what is it?

KATE. (*Offstage.*) Crane! Help! There's a man in my
room!

CRANE. I'm coming!

KATE. I'm being attacked!

VERNON. (*Runs downstairs in a panic.*) Helen! Helen!
Where are you? It isn't true. Heavens to Betsy, I'm not

a molester! (*Looks for somewhere to hide, opens the closet door but* RANDOLPH *is standing there.*)

RANDOLPH. This is taken!

VERNON. Excuse me! (*Closes door and runs out front door.*)

CRANE. (*Comes downstairs and puts on LIGHTS at foot of stairs.*) Kate, there's nothing here. Believe me, the room is empty. Come down and see for yourself.

KATE. (*Offstage.*) I'm frozen to this spot! (RANDOLPH *comes out of closet and sneaks quickly out French doors.*)

CRANE. Kate, you're just having a nightmare. It's all this talk about jewel thieves.

KATE. (*Comes down the stairs dressed in a bathrobe and a cap over her head to hide her curlers.* CRANE *is in a simple cotton dress.*) A man was in my room. A huge monster of a man.

CRANE. It's the excitement of finding two bodies in the closet. And then dropping off to sleep like that.

KATE. Crane, I tell you, I woke up and there was this Frankenstein in the room. A gigantic man with long arms like an ape. And fangs. Yes, I'm sure he had fangs. (*She indicates they are huge.*)

CRANE. See, Kate—nothing.

KATE. How about that closet?

CRANE. That's all in the past. We're here alone. (*Goes towards closet.*)

KATE. Crane—don't. I have a funny feeling.

CRANE. Nonsense. (*Opens closet door.*) See—empty.

KATE. Well—it's the first time tonight. What happened to our search party?

CRANE. I don't know. You slept and Lillian and Lyle never showed up.

KATE. Why don't you phone them?

CRANE. (*Crosses below* KATE *to phone and points at it.*) I'm having that thing ripped out in the morning. Mabel and I are no longer on speaking terms. That girl is a quiet drinker.

KATE. I warned you about her. Of course she drinks.

What else is there for her to do strapped to that switch-board like Cap'n Ahab to a whale?

CRANE. (*Starts to laugh.*) Do you suppose she makes her own in a still?

KATE. (*Laughing, too.*) And on every bottle she pastes a picture of Tallulah Bankhead.

CRANE. Let's start our search anyhow. I'll take upstairs and you start down here.

KATE. Oh, no! Not with that closet. (*Starts for stairs.*) I'll start upstairs.

CRANE. Have it your own way.

KATE. (*As she goes.*) If you hear a scream, it's only me—I hope.

(CRANE *looks around the room, decides on the sofa, examines the upholstery and feels behind the cush-ions, gives that up as a bad job and decides to try one of the doors. Starting at the French doors, she points them out, and, saying, "Eeny, meeny, mini, mo." The "mo" ends her up facing the kitchen door. She starts towards it and when she is almost there it opens and* PHILIP *is there holding his pistol.* CRANE *starts to scream.*)

PHILIP. Don't scream. I'm a friend.

CRANE. Honest? (*He nods.*) Scout's honor?

PHILIP. (*Gives scout's salute.*) Yes, ma'am.

CRANE. Well—who are you?

PHILIP. Mr. Hammond. I live here.

CRANE. You can't be Mr. Hammond.

PHILIP. But I am.

CRANE. No. I have a very good memory for faces and you definitely are not Mr. Hammond. I'm sure you're not. (*Looks closely at his face.*) No, you're not.

PHILIP. Who are you?

CRANE. Mrs. Hammond.

PHILIP. Oh, dear.

CRANE. Yes, oh, dear. What are you doing in my

house? (*Moves to phone.*) You tell me or I'll call that drunken operator and get that Zane Grey sheriff up here.

PHILIP. The operator's the one who told me I'm Mr. Hammond.

CRANE. Mabel did?

PHILIP. If that's the name of the voice in there.

CRANE. Maybe she takes dope, too.

PHILIP. I really am sorry to startle you like this.

CRANE. (*Warming up to him.*) Think nothing of it. (*Moves down to him.*) This evening is full of surprises. Now, by way of introduction, who are you?

PHILIP. That's just the point. I don't know.

CRANE. You can't be that forgetful. Everyone knows his own name. (*Gives a little squeal.*) Of course, that's who you are.

PHILIP. (*Grabs her by the shoulders.*) Who—tell me who—please!

CRANE. In there. You're the man who was hanging in my closet.

PHILIP. I know that, but who am I?

CRANE. You honestly don't know?

PHILIP. All I remember is that I was in some sort of a library for some reason and then I was hit from behind. Everything went like a kaleidoscope. In a way it was very pretty.

CRANE. You were in my library. Come with me. (*Opens closet door.*) We have a rather peculiar closet arrangement. It leads off this living room and off the library here. (*He follows her as she goes through into library.*) Is this the room you remember?

PHILIP. (*Offstage.*) This is it all right. I was standing over there when it happened. (*Comes back into the room and to below sofa.* CRANE *follows him in and closes the door.*) When I finally got clear enough to think, I was in some veterinarian's office.

CRANE. (*Crosses to him.*) That was Doc Parsons. I thought he was one of those wonderful old country M.D.'s. (*She sits on the sofa.*)

PHILIP. Maybe, but on his walls there were pictures of

horses and dogs and by his operating table there was a muzzle. So, when he was out of the room, I left and found my way back here. This is where it all started, so this is where I thought I must have lived.

CRANE. You have no idea who you were?

PHILIP. None at all. That operator told me I was Mr. Hammond when I spoke to some Indian person in Maine.

CRANE. That was my call to Kinni-Killi-Wock-Nock.

PHILIP. Well, it's your daughter's night off.

CRANE. Thanks. My woman's intuition says I can trust you. Sit down and let's figure out who you are. (*He sits beside her.*) Suppose you're the villain?

PHILIP. What villain?

CRANE. Somewhere here there are some stolen diamonds and everyone seems to be after them.

PHILIP. I don't think I'm a bad guy. Do I look bad?

CRANE. On the contrary—

PHILIP. Then I must be a good guy.

CRANE. Now for your name? Let's try a few on for size. Philip Smith?

PHILIP. No good. That's the name I made up when the Doc asked me.

CRANE. You don't look like a Philip. (*Rises and moves Center.*) James? Rock? John? Charles? Thomas?

PHILIP. This won't get us anywhere.

CRANE. (*Crosses above sofa Left.*) Were you happy at home?

PHILIP. I don't remember.

CRANE. Are you married?

PHILIP. (*Rises and faces front.*) That's it! Madeleine— it's coming back to me. Brown hair, dark eyes, short legs, and when she walks her tail wags. No, that's my dachshound. (*He sits again.*) Try again.

CRANE. (*Moves to Left of sofa.*) Sure you're not married?

PHILIP. I don't feel it.

CRANE. We'd better try another attack.

PHILIP. (*Jumps up.*) That's it!

CRANE. That's what?

PHILIP. Another attack!

CRANE. I meant verbal.

PHILIP. I didn't. If I lost my memory because someone hit me on the head, then shouldn't I get it back again with another hit?

CRANE. Possibly.

PHILIP. Do you have a blunt instrument?

CRANE. Not on me. Wait a minute. (*Crosses to desk and takes revolver from drawer where* LYLE *had put it.*) I have just the thing. I always use this in my books.

PHILIP. (*Moves in down Center.*) Are you Crane Hammond?

CRANE. There—you see, you do remember things.

PHILIP. Everything except who I am.

CRANE. (*Brings revolver to* PHILIP.) Here we are. Now hit yourself with the blunt end of this.

PHILIP. (*Reaches for it.*) Really?

CRANE. (*Pulls it back from him.*) This is stupid. If you are the Boss man, I shouldn't be handing you a gun. My readers would never believe it. But I'm sure I could trust anyone with a dachshound named Madeleine. (*Hands him the revolver.*)

PHILIP. (*Starts to hit himself. He lacks the courage however. Makes a second try. Puts the gun over his head and closes his eyes, but again lacks the courage. Hands the revolver to* CRANE *and sits in chair Center.*) Look, you hit me. I'm not masochistic enough to be brutal.

CRANE. I couldn't do that.

PHILIP. You've got to. It's my only chance.

CRANE. If you're sure. Where?

PHILIP. (*Points to the top of his head.*) Here.

CRANE. How hard?

PHILIP. Very. (*She draws back for a big hit.*) Wait! Mrs. Hammond, in case I remember everything and I'm a bad guy, I'll reform. You've been very nice to me.

CRANE. (*Smiles.*) Thank you.

PHILIP. O.K., shoot! I mean—hit! (CRANE *puts the butt of the revolver against the top of his head, closes her eyes, faces the other way and taps ever so slightly.* PHILIP *opens his eyes discouraged.*) Harder.

CRANE. In my books they do this all the time and it's no trouble. Ready? On your mark, get set, go! (*She brings the pistol down with great force, but since her eyes are closed, her aim is not too good and she swings above the chair, throwing herself off balance.*) I give up!

PHILIP. Maybe we could find a volunteer who isn't so kind-hearted.

CRANE. Let's see, who's around?

PHILIP. Everyone, I should think. There's an awful crowd of people milling outside and inside. I finally got a flashlight away from one woman so I could see what I was doing.

KATE. (*Comes downstairs.*) I couldn't even find a rhinestone. Have you found anything? (*At Up Center.*) Ohhh, you hit the jackpot! (*Notices that* CRANE *is holding the revolver pointing toward herself.*) You're holding the gun the wrong way! (*Turns it around and heads for the phone, going above* CRANE.) I'll call the police. (*She is now dressed in a summer cotton.*)

CRANE. No, Kate, this isn't who you think it is.

KATE. (*Comes down to* CRANE.) Then who is it?

CRANE. We're not sure *who* he is actually, but he's a good guy. Oh, this is Kate Bixley, my secretary. (PHILIP *rises.*) Kate, this is John Doe.

KATE. The face is familiar but the name escapes me.

PHILIP. How do you do?

CRANE. He has amnesia, but I'm sure we can trust him. He's trying to find out who he is.

KATE. This is no place to do it.

PHILIP. (*Exasperated, he crosses to below the sofa.*) Someone here must know me.

KATE. We're the only people in the house.

PHILIP. Are you kidding?

CRANE. He says people are everywhere like Red Square on May Day.

KATE. I suspected as much.

CRANE. I have an idea. (*Crosses to* PHILIP.) Phil Smith,

for want of a better name, will hide here and we'll go upstairs and put the lights out. Then, as a disinterested party, he can check on who is where and why.

KATE. I'm game for anything.

PHILIP. I don't know who I'm looking for.

CRANE. Neither do we.·

KATE. How about Lillian and Lyle?

CRANE. Oh, yes. We're expecting two people. They're friends. I mean they're friends *of ours*. They're married—to each other. Except that he's married to me—only for tonight, of course, until she gets her divorce and—oh, the hell with it! (*Hands him the revolver.*) Here, you take this.

PHILIP. Are you sure this is wise?

KATE. Peter Gunn would never do it.

CRANE. Hold up your index finger. (*He does.* CRANE *turns to* KATE.) See, Kate! Now, Phil, you just call if anything happens. We'll be ready. (*She starts upstairs followed by* KATE. PHILIP *is left looking at his index finger and wondering what it's all about.*) We can always use the extension phone upstairs.

KATE. To call who?

CRANE. Boston, I suppose. Of course we'll be dead of old age by the time Mabel gets a circuit.

KATE. I wonder if she's AC or DC. (*They are off.*)

(PHILIP *puts the gun in his pocket and looks around the room. He slowly approaches the closet and quickly opens the door but it is empty. He opens the kitchen door. As he is backing into the room,* LYLE *comes backing through the French doors. He is now dressed in slacks and a sport shirt. They bump Down Center.*)

LYLE AND PHILIP. What are you doing here? I'm Mr. Hammond. *You* are?

LYLE. This is rather embarrassing.

PHILIP. Yes, it is.

LYLE AND PHILIP. You see, I—

LYLE. Wait a minute. One at a time. I'll go first. Mr. Hammond, let me explain. I'm really Lillian Seymour's new husband and, well—Crane will explain why I was pretending to be you. My name is Lyle Rogers. (*Shakes* PHILIP'S *hand.*)

PHILIP. Oh, that makes everything clear.

LYLE. (*Starts for doors.*) I'll go get Lillian. I just wanted to be sure it was safe to bring her in.

PHILIP. It's perfectly safe.

LYLE. (*Comes back and pumps his hand.*) I sure am glad to meet you. Maybe you can straighten out this mess. Did you fly from Chicago for a surprise?

PHILIP. It's been an evening of surprises.

LYLE. Sure has. We'll be back in a couple of minutes.

(*He goes out leaving a bewildered* PHILIP. *As he backs upstage, the front door opens and* RANDOLPH *backs in. They collide at the arch Up Center.*)

PHILIP AND RANDOLPH. Who are you? I'm Mr. Hammond.

PHILIP. Now, just a   RANDOLPH. Cripes!
minute—

(RANDOLPH *runs out through French doors.* PHILIP *starts after him but decides to tell the girls upstairs what is happening. As he heads for the stairs the front door opens and* JENNY *rushes in.*)

JENNY. Randolph, wait for me. (*She collides with* PHILIP.) Oops!

JENNY AND PHILIP. Who are you? (JENNY *turns to windows and* PHILIP *up the stairs.*) Help!

CRANE. (*Offstage.*) Coming.

KATE. (*Offstage.*) Hang on.

PHILIP. (*Struggling with* JENNY.) What are you doing sneaking in here?

JENNY. I work here.

PHILIP. What's your name?

JENNY. Jenny.

CRANE. (*Comes downstairs followed by* KATE.) What's going on here? Jenny, you went home hours ago.

JENNY. (*Crosses below* PHILIP *to* CRANE.) I come back to cook breakfast.

KATE. (*As she shuts the front door.*) At two in the morning?

JENNY. Is that what time it is? My clock broke. I thought it must be time to get up. I heard a cock crow.

CRANE. That was Miss Bixley screaming. (KATE *moves to above the desk.*) Jenny, this is Mr. Smith. He's a very dear friend of ours.

JENNY. He looks familiar. Ain't I seen you somewhere before?

PHILIP. Nooo!

CRANE. (*Pushes* JENNY *towards the kitchen.*) Now that you're here, why don't you go in the kitchen and make some coffee or something? I think we're up for the day.

JENNY. Yes'm. I don't know if I'll work here much longer, though. I don't approve of the goin's on. (*She slams out.*)

CRANE. (*To* PHILIP.) You'd better get out there and keep an eye on her.

PHILIP. (*As he starts for kitchen.*) Am I supposed to trust her?

CRANE. Trust no one, not even yourself till you find out who you are. (*This stops* PHILIP *momentarily at the door, then he goes out.*)

KATE. My next vacation, I'm going to pitch a pup tent in Times Square and just relax.

CRANE. This will all pass, Kate, like scarlet fever. (*DOORBELL rings.*) Now what?

JENNY. (*Enters.*) Am I supposed to answer the door this early in the morning?

CRANE. I will do it. (*She opens the front door, gives a screech and slams it shut and leans against it. A man's arm is caught in the door and it waves about.* NOTE: *If the actor playing the man puts his foot in the door, it will keep the door open enough so the pressure won't be on his arm.*) Jenny, go—go—go back into the kitchen.

JENNY. (*Indicating the waving arm.*) Someone wants to get in.

CRANE. Kate!

KATE. Jenny, go or I shall practice my ju-jitsu! (*She takes the pose and starts after* JENNY *who flees to the kitchen.* KATE *moves up on the Left side of the desk.*) What is it?

CRANE. Look! (*Opens the door and* RICHARD HAMMOND *stumbles in. He carries a briefcase and wears a hat and dark traveling suit. He is somewhat older than* CRANE *and a typically nice-looking businessman.*)

RICHARD. Surprise, I think!

KATE. Mr. Hammond!

CRANE. (*Throws her arms around him.*) Richard, darling, how sweet of you.

RICHARD. Did I pick a wrong moment?

CRANE. (*As she closes front door.*) Any moment this evening would have been wrong. But aren't you in Chicago?

RICHARD. I quit the conference and flew back.

CRANE. Quit?

RICHARD. (*Very pleased with this announcement, he crosses out of the arch, below* CRANE *and to below the closet.*) And I resigned from the newspaper. The novel's been accepted and I'm getting a healthy advance. What do you think of that?

CRANE. (*Embracing*   KATE. Congratulations,
him.) Darling.   Mr. Hammond.

KATE. Crane, what if he's found here?

CRANE. Oh, yes. Richard, now don't ask for explanations. It's so silly, but—

(*The front door opens and* VERNON *pokes his head in. He cannot see* RICHARD *and* CRANE *standing below the closet.* CRANE *pushes* RICHARD *in the closet, closes the door and leans against it.*)

VERNON. Evenin', Miss Bixley.

CRANE. Why, Verne, what are you doing up at this hour?

VERNON. (*Moves down to* CRANE. KATE *slowly crosses to kitchen door till she is standing guard over that.*) I just discovered a car out front—one of them you-rent-it things. The receipt inside says it's made out to a Mr. Richard Hammond; said it was hired five hours ago in Boston and we know Mr. Hammond was sittin' here five hours ago. I think someone's impersonatin' your husband.

CRANE. I don't believe it, do you, Kate?

KATE. Nooo!

VERNON. I think we oughta have a talk with your husband.

CRANE. Not now. Wait till the morning.

VERNON. Everyone seems to be awake. I think we oughta talk now. (*He goes to the foot of the stairs and calls up.*) Mr. Hammond!

(RICHARD *pushes open the closet door and* CRANE, *leaning against it, pushes him back. At the same time the business goes on between* KATE *and* PHILIP.)

VERNON. Did you hear something?

KATE AND CRANE. Nothing at all.

VERNON. I think I did. (*Calls again.*) Mr. Hammond! (*Repeat of door pushing business.*) You two women are concealing something, all right.

(*The front door bursts open and a very dishevelled* HELEN *comes in. Her purse is gone, her hat is over one eye, and her hair is a mess. She staggers to the Right side of the arch and collapses against it.*)

HELEN. I have been attacked!

VERNON. Helen!

HELEN. I was grabbed from behind. Someone stole my flashlight and left me flat in the rhododendrons.

CRANE. I didn't know we had rhododendrons.

HELEN. And prickly roses.

PHILIP. (*Comes out from the kitchen.*) Cream with your coffee?

HELEN. (*Points at* PHILIP.) That's him. That's the attacker.

CRANE. (*Indicating doors.*) Run! (PHILIP *rushes out.*)

HELEN. Get him, Verne. He's Redfax's boss. (VERNON *runs after* PHILIP *and* HELEN *runs out after* VERNON.)

CRANE. (*Opens closet door.* RICHARD *is standing there leaning against the jamb. Politely, as though nothing had happened.*) Darling, you must think this is very peculiar.

RICHARD. Crane, what is happening?

CRANE. Kate, you watch Jenny.

KATE. With pleasure. (*She goes out to the kitchen, rolling up her sleeve on the way.*)

CRANE. Darling, there's some kind of a mix-up with people and bodies and diamonds.

RICHARD. You're writing another book?

CRANE. This one has sort of gotten out of hand. I'll explain. (*She moves away Down Left.*) There are some diamonds here and it seems there are several people after them. (*The closet door opens and* RANDOLPH *comes out, hits* RICHARD *on the back of the head with the butt of his gun and shoves* RICHARD *in the closet and closes the door. He moves to above* CRANE *pointing the gun at her.*) A fence, who is the big boss, and some hoodlums, and then there's this private eye in the crowd somewhere. (*She moves Right and* RANDOLPH *follows above her.*) But the whole thing got mixed up because Lillian married Lyle and he has to pretend to be my husband because she got divorced in Mexico. But I don't care about all that. You're here now and I love you and— (*Turns around and stares right into the muzzle of the gun. She drops in a dead faint.* RANDOLPH *runs out the front door as we hear* LILLIAN *calling outside French doors, "Crane! Crane!"*)

LILLIAN. (*Enters and sees* CRANE *lying on the floor.*) What happened? (*Crosses to the Left of* CRANE.) Did you find another body? Crane!

(*As she pats her hand, voices are heard outside front door and* RANDOLPH *comes in, runs between chair and sofa and jumps over* CRANE. *The others repeat this business in order:* PHILIP, VERNON, *and* HELEN. *As each jumps over* CRANE, LILLIAN *tries to get his attention. As the last goes out French doors,* KATE *enters from kitchen.*)

KATE. Is there a stampede? It sounds like a rerun of "Ben Hur." (CRANE *starts to come to.*)
LILLIAN. She's coming to. (*Moves to Right of* CRANE.)
KATE. What happened, another body? (*Moves to her Left.*)
CRANE. Richard. Richard.
LILLIAN. She's delirious.
KATE. No, Richard's here. (*Looks around.*) Somewhere.
CRANE. Richard, where are you?
LILLIAN. Crane, dear, there are hordes of people running through your house like it was the Indianapolis Speedway.
KATE. Come on, now, can you stand?
CRANE. (*As they help her up.*) Of course. I was talking to Richard and suddenly he changed into another person right in front of my eyes, like Jekyll and Hyde.
LILLIAN. Crane, you're delirious.
LYLE. (*Appears at doors.*) Lillian, there you are. There's a regular track meet going on out there.
LILLIAN. I know, dear. (*There is a GROAN from the closet.* LILLIAN *rushes to* LYLE *and* KATE *backs over to desk.*) Who's that?
KATE. Quasimodo!
CRANE. Richard, darling. (*She opens the closet door just as* RICHARD *is getting to his feet. He comes out.*)
RICHARD. (*Rubbing his head.*) I'm going back to Chicago.
LILLIAN. Richard, how wonderful of you to come.
JENNY. (*Enters from the kitchen with the familiar bucket of ice.*) Ice!
KATE. I'll make drinks. (*Takes bucket up to bar.*)

JENNY. (*Pointing at* RICHARD.) Who's that?

CRANE. This is my husband, Jenny.

JENNY. (*Pointing at* LYLE.) Then who's that?

CRANE. Oh, never mind. Just go make breakfast—do something.

JENNY. I could sell this whole story to Confidential. (*She slams out to the kitchen.*)

CRANE. (*Sitting* RICHARD *on the Right side of the sofa and sitting beside him.*) Richard, you come and sit down here and rest your head.

RICHARD. Someone hit me.

CRANE. I know, dear.

RICHARD. Aren't you upset?

CRANE. Well, everyone else has been through it already.

LILLIAN. Can anyone explain the whole thing to anyone?

KATE. Here. (*Hands drinks to* CRANE *and* RICHARD *and returns to the bar for her own drink.*)

CRANE. Thanks.

LILLIAN. First, Richard, I'd like you to meet my husband. You see, Crane borrowed him for a while or rather I insisted she take him and that started it all.

LYLE. I couldn't get back to our home for a while because Vernon Cookley—

RICHARD. You mean you stayed here?

LYLE. It was rather an unusual arrangement for a honeymoon. But Kate was here.

KATE. (*Turning from bar, with a smile.*) Yes, I fell asleep.

RICHARD. What! (KATE *turns back to bar.*)

CRANE. (*Rises.*) Stop everything! Right this minute. I know where the diamonds are and we might as well settle this whole thing. (*Crosses to front door.*)

KATE. You know?   ⎫
LILLIAN. Where?   ⎬ (*Together.*)
LYLE. You found them? ⎭

CRANE. (*Leaning out the front door.*) Hello, out there! Come on in! Everyone out of the pool!

KATE. Where are they?

CRANE. (*Moves to the Right of the arch.*) Close the doors, Lyle. (*He does and puts on the bolt.* LILLIAN *fades down to him.*)

LILLIAN. Where are the diamonds?

CRANE. Here they come. Stand aside! (PHILIP *runs in first, followed by* VERNON *and finally* HELEN. *They are all yelling at one another. When* PHILIP *gets to the doors, he stops and they pile up against him.*) Now, be quiet. Quiet! *Quiet!* (*They suddenly stop talking.*) That's better. Now let's all sit down like ladies and gentlemen and I'll explain this whole mess.

(*There is a general ad-lib as they settle around the room:* HELEN *sits in chair Center,* VERNON *moves to above her,* KATE *sits in the desk chair and puts her drink on the desk,* PHILIP *to above the sofa and* LILLIAN *and* LYLE *by the doors.*)

VERNON. You know something?

CRANE. Enough. The first problem to settle is where are the diamonds? Simple! The ice is in the ice. (*Holds up her glass.*) Inside each ice cube is a diamond or two. (*General ad-lib.*)

KATE. (*Picking up her glass.*) What about the drinks we had this afternoon? Have I swallowed a gem?

CRANE. I guess that tray was empty but the others are loaded.

(*Closet door opens and* RANDOLPH *comes out and hits* PHILIP *over the head.* PHILIP *collapses on the back of the sofa.*)

RANDOLPH. Hands up everyone! I'll take those! (RICHARD *rises and fades Right.*)

RICHARD. Crane, are these all house guests?

RANDOLPH. I'll take the ice, lady.

(PHILIP *shakes himself out of it, grabs the gun from*

RANDOLPH *and in one quick move, throws him to
the floor.*)

PHILIP. O.K., boy, you've had it.
RANDOLPH. (*Almost crying.*) No, that's cheating. I
almost had the ice.
PHILIP. You'll be cool enough where you're going.
And thanks for the hit on the head.
RANDOLPH. You nuts or something?
CRANE. You remember?
PHILIP. Sure do.
LILLIAN. Isn't that the body?
LYLE. Philip Smith!
VERNON. Now one crook loses and another crook wins.
JENNY. (*Enters from kitchen with a revolver. She now
drops her country accent and ways and becomes very
efficient.*) All right, everyone. Hands up! (RANDOLPH
gets up and scrambles above the sofa. HELEN *rises.*)
CRANE. Jenny!
JENNY. I'll take the diamonds if you don't mind.
PHILIP. (*Moves Down Right Center.*) No. I was here
first.
JENNY. (*Moves in to* PHILIP.) But I have the author-
ity.
JENNY AND PHILIP. (*As the muzzles of their guns
meet.*) You're under arrest!
PHILIP. I'm a private detective from Boston hired by
the insurance company.
JENNY. And I'm from Pinkerton's. We've been trailing
this man since June.
VERNON. (*Crosses down to above them.*) What about
the local constabulary?
JENNY. Shall we all work together?
VERNON AND PHILIP. (*As all* THREE *shake hands.*)
Agreed!
KATE. But who's the Boss if you're all the good guys?
CRANE. Haven't you figured that out yet?
RANDOLPH. I'm not talkin'.
CRANE. (*Moves Up Center.*) That's a simple matter.

Always take the enemy by surprise. (*Calls in a sharp and loud voice.*) Hey, Boss!

HELEN. (*One hand automatically goes to her hip, and in a low, common voice she snaps back.*) Yeah! (*All in the room freeze, HELEN realizes her mistake and her hand goes to her mouth.*)

RANDOLPH. Boss, you gave it away!

CRANE. Why, Miss O'Toole.

PHILIP. Good work, Mrs. Hammond. And you, too, Miss—

JENNY. Myra Crandall.

VERNON. (*Moves above HELEN.*) And I thought you was helpin' me.

HELEN. (*In her tough voice. Crosses Up to CRANE.*) I come all the way up here to this Sunnybrook Farm, set myself up as a real estate agent for a front, and all for what? (*Moves Down to desk and picks up KATE's drink.*) Caught by the Bobsey Twins! (*Slugs down the drink.*)

VERNON. And I thought it was Mrs. Hammond. (*Moves to CRANE.*)

JENNY. I thought it was you, Verne. You're too good to be true.

VERNON. That's why I'm sheriff.

JENNY. I played along with Randolph but he wouldn't give away who the boss was.

VERNON. Everyone get your flashlight and your gun and we'll clear out. These poor people haven't had a chance to see how peaceful it is in Birchville.

(JENNY *heads for the kitchen door and* RANDOLPH *starts to sneak out the open closet door.*)

LILLIAN. Look, Lyle!

LYLE. (*Grabs* RANDOLPH, *pulls him back in the room and closes the closet door.*) No, you don't! Better stay here!

VERNON. (*To* PHILIP.) Better keep an eye on them, young fella. (*Exits to library.*)

PHILIP. Yes, Mr. Sheriff! Come on, you. (RANDOLPH

moves over to the Left of the arch above the desk.) Get over there, O'Toole.

HELEN. (*As she joins* RANDOLPH *and* PHILIP *Up Left.*) Drop dead!

RICHARD. (*Hoping for an explanation.*) Crane, will you please—

CRANE. (*Remembers he is there. Brightly.*) Oh, Richard. (*Crosses down to him.*) I think you know the least about the most and I know the most about the most so I'd better explain. We arrived this afternoon and Lillian had her husband hide in the closet for a joke. Being the scare-easy type, I fainted, but later there was another body. Well, you see— (*She moves to the closet.*) I went over and opened the door and—

(*Opens the closet door and there is a figure there. Once again,* CRANE *falls in a dead faint. The body turns out to be* VERNON, *he is holding a huge book in front of his face. He lowers the book, looks at* CRANE *and speaks.*)

VERNON. I was just borrowin' a book!

(EVERYONE *holds in a tableau as:*)

THE CURTAIN FALLS

PROPERTY LIST

ACT ONE

On Stage:
Silent butler on what-not shelf
Large fake, gingham flower with card attached on desk
Bottles of liquor, including Scotch, brandy, creme de menthe
  on bar
Glasses on bar
Cigarettes and ash trays on table by sofa and table by chair
  Center
Off Right:
Purse (LILLIAN)
Off Up Center:
Purse with pencil and pad in it (KATE)
Briefcase (KATE)
Purse (CRANE)
Luggage, several pieces including hat box (VERNE)
Sheriff's badge (VERNE)
Off Up Right (Library):
Copy of "Little Women" (CRANE)
Off Left:
Ice tray from refrigerator (JENNY)
Old paint bucket with ice in it (JENNY)

ACT TWO

Clear glasses to bar
Ash tray sofa table filled
Coffee cups (4) on tray at desk (JENNY)
Ice bucket refilled
Off Up Center: (Upstairs)
Hot water bottle (KATE)
Off Left:
Coffee pot full (JENNY)
Off Up Center: (Outside)
Revolver (VERNON)
Off Up Right (Library):
Copy of "War and Peace" (CRANE)
Copy of another book (CRANE)

ACT THREE

Strike ice bucket
Clear glasses to bar

Off Right:
Flashlight (HELEN)
Flashlight (VERNON)
Off Up Center (outside) :
Briefcase (RICHARD)
Off Up Right (Library) :
Copy of "The Raven" (CRANE)
Copy of "The White Cliffs" (CRANE)
Revolver (RANDOLPH)
Large book (VERNON)
Off Left:
Flashlight (JENNY)
Handkerchief (RANDOLPH)
Instruction book (RANDOLPH)
Ice bucket from previous act filled (JENNY)
Revolver (JENNY)

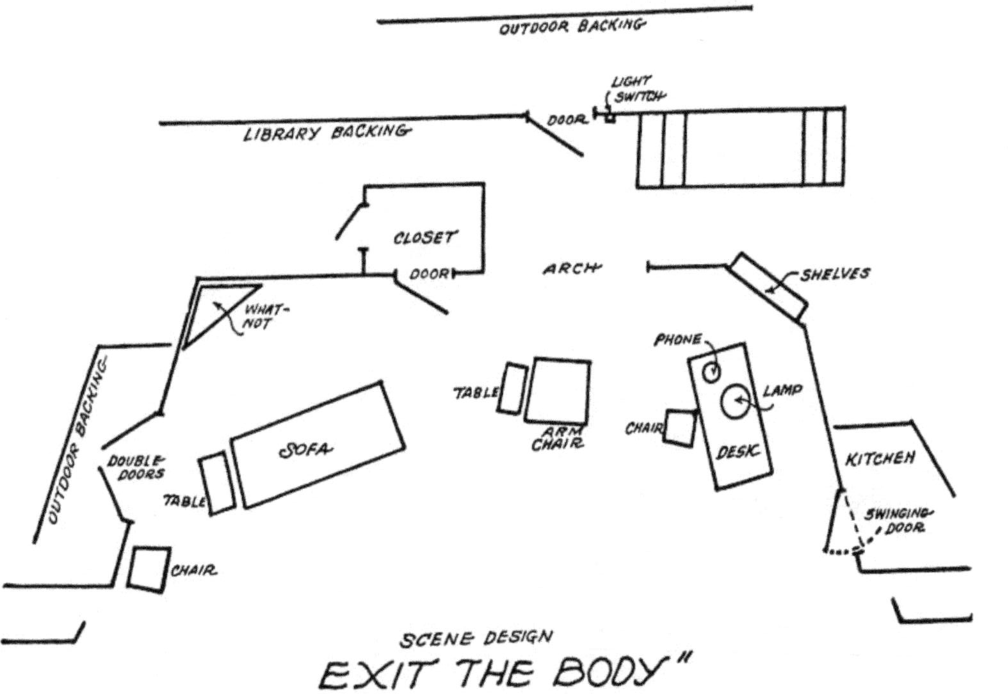

OUTDOOR BACKING
LIBRARY BACKING
LIGHT SWITCH
DOOR
CLOSET
DOOR
ARCH
SHELVES
WHAT-NOT
OUTDOOR BACKING
PHONE
LAMP
DESK
CHAIR
TABLE
ARM CHAIR
SOFA
DOUBLE DOORS
TABLE
CHAIR
KITCHEN
SWINGING-DOOR
SCENE DESIGN
EXIT THE BODY"

Also by
Fred Carmichael...

All the Better to Kill You
  With

Any Number Can Die

The Best Laid Plans

Coming Apart

Damsel of the Desert or A
  Villain Foiled By Virtue

Decisions, Decisions

Don't Mention My Name

Don't Step on My Footprint

Done to Death

Double in Diamonds

Dream World

Exit Who?

Foiled By an Innocent Maid

Frankenstein 1930

Guess Who's Coming to
  Lunch (Or Just Desserts)

He's Having a Baby

Hey, Naked Lady

Home Free

Hot Property

I Bet Your Life

Inside Lester

Last of the Class

Luxury Cruise

Meet My Husbands

Mixed Doubles

More Than Meets the Eye

Murder Go Round

Murder is a Game

Murder on the Rerun

The Night is My Enemy

Out of Sight... Out of
  Murder

Over the Checkerboard

P is for Perfect

The Pen is Deadlier

Petey's Choice

The Robin Hood Caper

Said the Spider to the Spy

So Nice Not to See You

Surprise!

Ten Nights in a Bar Room

The Three Million Dollar
  Lunch

The Trouble With Trent

Victoria's House

What If ...?

Whatever Happened to Mrs.
  Kong?

Who Needs a Waltz

Please visit our website **samuelfrench.com** for complete
descriptions and licensing information.

OTHER TITLES AVAILABLE FROM SAMUEL FRENCH

THE PEN IS DEALIER

Fred Carmichael

All Groups / Mystery / 4m, 6f / Int.

This exciting mystery contains two murders with ever mounting excitement and explores the fascinating psychological overtones and undertones that impel the murder to the crime. Atop one of the fashionable Hollywood Hills, Clair Clarendon, top gossip columnist, reigns supreme over her helpless targets. Their lives and loves are ruled by her pen and it is not surprising that all of them could wish her dead. Ideal for college and little theatre groups, and recommended for advanced high school drama clubs as it provides superb acting assignments for the whole cast, plus a challenging directing job. Audiences attending this play's premiere performances at the Dorset Playhouse, Vermont, were loud and long in their applause.